Witch Catcher

Mary Downing Hahn

sandpiper

Houghton Mifflin Harcourt

Boston New York

Originally published in hardcover in the United States by Clarion Books,
an imprint of Houghton Mifflin Harcourt Publishing Company, 2006.

www.hmhbooks.com

The Library of Congress has cataloged the hardcover edition as follows:
Hahn, Mary Downing
Witch catcher / by Mary Downing Hahn
p. cm.
Summary: Having just moved into the West Virginia home they inherited from a distant relative, twelve-year-old Jen is surprised that her father is already dating a local antiques dealer, but more surprised by what the spooky woman really wants.
[1. Witches—Fiction. 2. Fairies—Fiction. 3. Fathers and daughters—Fiction. 4. Single-parent families—Fiction. 5. Cats—Fiction. 6. West Virginia—Fiction.]
I. Title.
PZ7.H1256Wit 2006
[Fic]—dc22
2005024795

ISBN-13: 978-0-618-50457-2 hardcover
ISBN-13: 978-0-547-57714-2 paperback

Manufactured inthe United States of America
DOC 10 9 8 7 6 5 4 3 2 1

4500307013

For my neighbors,
Kathleen and Sarah,
who love to read

"THERE IT IS, JEN." Dad slowed the van and pointed at a big stone house high on a hill above the road. "Mostyn Castle. Our new home, thanks to Great-Uncle Thaddeus, bless his strange old soul."

I leaned out the window and stared up, up, up, stretching my neck to see above the treetops. Months ago, when Dad told me about the house, I'd accused him of exaggerating, but for once he'd told the truth. It really *was* built like a castle, turrets and all. Crowning the hilltop, dark and mysterious, the house was a place where anything could happen—anything except the ordinary.

"It's a big change from what you're used to," Dad said quietly. "Nobody next door. Nobody across the street. No friends nearby. Just you and me rattling around in dozens of big, dark rooms."

"I love it." I leaned back in my seat and grinned. A castle—I was going to live in a castle, a childhood wish come true.

"If you're not happy here," he went on, "we'll sell it and move back home to Maryland."

I turned and watched cloud shadows pattern the castle's stone walls. "I'll be happy," I promised him. "And so will Tink."

At the sound of his name, my cat meowed impatiently from his cage in the back seat. I reached around and touched his pink nose with the tip of my finger. "We're almost there," I told him.

"Tink will be ecstatic," Dad said. "Can you imagine how many mice he'll catch?"

Without thinking, I asked, "What about my mother? Would she have liked living here?"

"Yes, I think so." Dad gripped the steering wheel a little too tightly. "Elaine loved castles and fairy tales, magic. . . ." His voice drifted off and he gazed at the castle, seeing it with my mother's eyes, I thought. Seeing it for her.

While he sat there silently, I watched a fly buzz against the inside of the windshield. To me, my mother was a face in a photo, a character in an unfinished story, someone who died before I was old enough to remember her. But I missed her as much as Dad did, needed her as much as he did, loved her as much as he did.

"I just wondered—" I broke off with an embarrassed shrug, sorry I'd spoiled the mood of the day.

Dad eased the van into gear. "We'd better get going," he said. "We have a lot to do." Soon a wall of trees blocked our view of the house.

"Tell me about Uncle Thaddeus," I said. "Did you ever meet him?"

"Once," he said. "I must have been five or six. We happened to be passing through this part of West Virginia on our way home from a vacation, and my father suggested paying Uncle Thaddeus a visit. He thought the old man would enjoy meeting me."

Dad shook his head in remembrance. "Great-Uncle Thaddeus was the scariest person I'd ever seen. Tall and gaunt, long white beard, old-fashioned black suit. He didn't smile or say one word to me the whole time we were there, but he watched every move I made. The place was full of antiques—valuable stuff, according to my mother. Vases, statues, bric-a-brac. He must have been worried I'd break something. I was convinced he hated me."

I looked at Dad, puzzled. "But he left his house to you. He must have liked you."

"Uncle Thaddeus died without a will, Jen. Apparently, I'm his only living relative, so the court awarded his estate to me. Who knows what the old man wanted to happen to his property?"

Dad turned right into a curving driveway lined with tall, drooping trees whose branches scraped the roof of our van. I caught sight of squirrels dashing this way and that, alarmed by the engine's noise. Birds flew out of the trees, fluttering about in confusion. I thought I glimpsed a deer streaking away through the underbrush.

The driveway ended in a weedy circle in front of the house. Steep steps rose to a porch, and beyond them were two massive wooden doors, their panels carved with twining vines and leaves. Crouching stone lions flanked the steps, their snarling faces furrowed from years of rain and snow. Trailing long strands of ivy, a pair of tall stone urns stood on either side of the door.

In spite of the summer sun, I shivered. Up close, the house was not as inviting as it had appeared from a distance.

Dad shoved a huge key into the lock and, with some effort, opened the doors. Lugging Tink's cage, I followed him into a dark hallway that smelled of dusty air and cold stone. In the kitchen, I put Tink's cage on the floor. He cowered inside, meowing pitifully.

"I'll set you free when we get settled," I told him. "If I open the door now, you might run outside and get lost."

Tink made himself as small as possible in the very back of his cage and continued to meow in a plaintive, kittenish way. He was a big yellow tabby but very timid. The original scaredy-cat.

"Don't worry," I told him. "We're not at the vet's office. Nobody's going to take your temperature or give you a shot. This is our new home."

Tink meowed louder and twitched his tail.

"I'm beginning to think you don't like it here," I said softly.

"Jen," Dad called from the hall. "I could use some help."

I reached into the cage, gave Tink a pat on his nose, and left him to fuss in private.

Dad and I made trip after trip to the van and back, carrying in our luggage, a few days' supply of groceries, our books, clothes, and other personal stuff. We didn't need anything else. The house was crammed with Uncle Thaddeus's belongings—tables and chairs, beds and bureaus, sideboards and sofas, armchairs and clocks, books and bookcases; enough furniture to fill all the houses in a city block.

Before I unpacked, I carried Tink to the room I'd chosen for myself, just down the hall from Dad's. I closed the door and let him out of his cage. He immediately ran under the bed and refused to budge.

I got down on the floor and tried to lure him out, but he'd pushed himself against the far wall. He crouched there and stared at me, as if to ask why I'd brought him here.

"Okay," I told him. "Stay there."

I got to my feet and went to the window to see what I could see from my room. I drew in a deep breath, amazed at the sight of a tall stone tower behind the house. Weeds and brambles had grown up around its base, and its walls were almost hidden by ivy. The afternoon sun glinted on tiny windows under the eaves of the roof. Rapunzel, Sleeping Beauty, Bluebeard's wife—any of them could be imprisoned there.

Leaving Tink huddled under the bed, I ran downstairs to find Dad. "There's a tower in the backyard," I cried. "Have you seen it?"

He looked up from a box of groceries. "I've been to the house four or five times already. How could I have missed something as big as that tower?"

"Why didn't you tell me about it?" Without giving him a chance to answer, I shot out the door and ran down the hill toward the tower.

Behind me Dad called, "Jen, wait!"

But I was too excited to stop. I plunged through the weeds and bushes and stopped in front of a huge oak door carved with strange marks—not exactly words, not exactly pictures, but symbols of some sort. Despite the rusty padlock, I tugged at the door, but I couldn't budge it.

Dad crashed through the bushes behind me.

"The door's locked," I told him. "Do you have the key?"

"Yes," he said, "but I plan to keep it locked."

I stared at him in surprise. "Why?"

"I explored the place on my first visit. The stairs are rotting, and the floors are unsound. I didn't dare go to the top. All that's holding those stone walls together is ivy. One good wind could topple the whole thing like a pile of blocks."

"But, Dad, don't you want to know what's up there?" I gazed at the tiny windows catching the late-afternoon sun and imagined treasure hidden under the floorboards.

Shading his eyes, Dad squinted at the tower. "Anything Uncle Thaddeus left behind would be ruined by now. Most of the windows are broken. The roof leaks. I'm sure bats, pigeons, and mice have done their share of damage, as well as years of rain and snow."

"Couldn't we at least go see?" Although I wasn't fond of bats, pigeons, or mice, I wanted to climb the rotting stairs to the very top. I wanted to look out those little windows and see the woods and the house and the gardens from way up high. But most of all I wanted to find something wonderful tucked out of sight in an old chest. A treasure, maybe—gold coins, jewels, silver . . . things worthy of being locked away in an old tower.

Dad tugged on the padlock to make sure it was locked. "The tower's not safe," he repeated. "It's strictly off-limits to you."

I bit my lip to keep from begging. Dad didn't like me to argue with him. If I backed off now, he might change his mind later.

When he started to turn away, I grabbed his arm. "Did you notice these?" I pointed at the odd marks on the door.

Dad studied the carvings. "They look like runes. Ancient writing, supposedly the language of magic and spells."

"Why would your uncle carve them on the door? They're spooky."

Dad shrugged. "Apparently, Great-Uncle Thaddeus was a strange man, Jen. He lived here like a hermit. Never went anywhere, never entertained. A recluse, but harmless—more eccentric than anything else."

Dad looked at the runes again. "According to the lawyer who settled the estate, my uncle had quite a reputation in town. People mistrusted him. They spoke of seeing lights in the tower windows every night till dawn. It was rumored that he never slept, never ate, never spoke. A few even suspected he practiced witchcraft."

Despite the warm June day, goose bumps pimpled my skin. "Do you think it's true, Dad?"

“Of course not.” Dad glanced up at the house. The sun was behind it now, darkening the stonework. “Great-Uncle Thaddeus was a brilliant man, a scholar, an artist, a gardener, a philosopher. He didn’t fit in with the locals, so they made up ridiculous stories about him.” He frowned. “It’s the fate of extraordinary people to be misunderstood by ordinary people.”

I’d heard Dad state this opinion many times before. He was an artist himself, forced to teach high school art classes for a living. Most of the time he made a joke out of it—the poor starving artist breaking up fights in the school parking lot. But on bad days he complained he was unappreciated, misunderstood, undervalued. Mom had been good at getting him to laugh at himself, Dad always said. Too bad I didn’t have her talent.

While Dad nattered away about small towns and small minds, I reached out and touched one of the runes on the door. For a moment, I felt an odd tingling, almost like a tiny shock. Startled, I jerked my hand back.

I glanced at Dad to see if he’d noticed, but he was already walking up the hill toward the house. I followed him slowly, glancing back now and then at the tower. The ivy on its walls rustled in the breeze, rising and falling as if the tower were alive and breathing. High up, the tiny windows sparkled in the sunlight.

With or without Dad’s permission, I planned to explore the tower the first chance I got.

2

I CAUGHT UP WITH Dad in the kitchen, where he stood staring helplessly at the pots and pans he'd been attempting to organize before I interrupted him.

"It's almost time for dinner, and I can't find anything," he said.

Tink jumped up on the counter and accidentally knocked a pile of lids to the floor. Dad swatted at him in annoyance. "Get down!"

Giving Dad a disdainful look, the cat ignored him. His fears forgotten, Tink had definitely made himself at home. Tail waving, he prowled the counter, weaving his way through the clutter, sniffing this, sniffing that, looking in vain for supper.

"Maybe we should just go out for pizza," Dad muttered.

"Where would we get it?" I asked. "Mingo's the nearest town, and it's at least twenty-five miles away."

Dad sighed. "We're not in the suburbs anymore, are we? No mall, no fast-food places, no pizza delivery. In other words, if we want pizza, we'll have to make it ourselves." He rummaged through a carton of groceries and came up with a package of pizza mix.

"Yuck." I scowled at the grinning chef on the front of the box. "Not *that* stuff, Dad."

"You can always make yourself a peanut butter sandwich," he said cheerfully.

While I fed Tink, Dad busied himself with the pizza. Even though he was a pretty good cook, I didn't have much hope for the sticky white dough he was smothering with canned tomato sauce. Tink showed no interest in it. Usually he preferred our food to his, but tonight he seemed perfectly happy with his Kitty Delight chopped sardines.

When the pizza was ready, Dad insisted we eat in the dining room—much more special, he said, than the kitchen, especially for our first meal in Great-Uncle Thaddeus's house. The two of us sat at one end of a table that must have been at least twelve feet long. To my surprise, the pizza smelled almost as good as the real thing and tasted better than I'd expected—or maybe I was just too hungry to be picky.

After we'd finished eating, we lingered at the table. Here in the mountains, the heat faded with the setting sun. To drive off the evening chill, Dad had gotten a small fire going in the hearth, and I'd lit dozens of candles, but the room was far from cozy. It was too big, for one thing, high-ceilinged and filled with shadows. Long velvet drapes hid the windows, and dark oil paintings in ornate frames tilted out from the walls. Great-Uncle Thaddeus seemed to have had a taste for desolate landscapes, gloomy still lifes, and portraits of pale, frowning people who no doubt disapproved of pizza.

Tink brushed against my legs, purring like a motor running at full speed. It comforted me to know he was there, so close, so warm and soft.

"Is Great-Uncle Thaddeus in any of those pictures?" I asked.

Dad scanned the portraits. "There's the jolly old soul." He pointed at a painting of a white-haired man with a beard. Uncle Thaddeus's face was long and thin, his cheeks were pale, and he had no twinkle in his eye. His expression was decidedly unfriendly.

"A self-portrait, I think," Dad said. "He was a good painter."

"I guess that's where you got your talent." I tilted my head and studied the painting. "He looks exactly like you described him. I'd be scared of him, too."

Dad laughed. "Even in a painting, he has a certain commanding presence."

"I wouldn't want that picture hanging on my bedroom wall," I said. "I'd never get any sleep with him staring down at me."

"Well, no matter what the old boy was like or how he'd feel about us living here," Dad said, "I salute him for giving me the opportunity to become a man of leisure."

Raising his coffee cup, Dad got to his feet. "To Great-Uncle Thaddeus, who unwittingly saved me from twenty more years of teaching art to Philistines."

"A toast, a toast!" I raised my water glass. "Hip, hip, hooray for Great-Uncle Thaddeus, the king of Mostyn Castle!"

"Hear, hear." Dad's voice echoed in the high-ceilinged room.

Swallowing the last of his coffee, he began gathering our plates. "Let's clean up, Jen. It's been a long day for both of us."

After we'd cleared the table and washed the dishes, I picked up Tink. "Are you going to bed now?" I asked Dad.

"I think I'll read for a while first," he said. "You run along. I'll be up soon."

Taking Tink with me, I climbed the long flight of steps to the second floor and walked down the hall to my room.

Before I got into bed, I looked out the window at the tower. In the moonlight it looked even more mysterious. "What do you suppose Great-Uncle Thaddeus did up there all night long?" I whispered to Tink.

He looked at me, amber eyes glowing, and touched my face gently with his paw.

"You're a cat," I reminded him. "You *must* be curious."

Tink blinked. Leaping from my arms, he ran to the bed and jumped on the pillow, his favorite sleeping place. Looking at me pointedly, he meowed loudly. It was time for bed. If I didn't get under those covers soon, he'd start fussing at me.

I lingered a moment at the window. The leaves in the big oak near the house stirred and rustled. The moon shone down on fields and woods, casting the tower's long black shadow toward the house. The stars seemed thicker and brighter, closer somehow without streetlights and neon signs and headlights.

Tink mewed several times, reminding me again it was time for bed. The breeze coming through the window was cool, and I was glad to snuggle under the covers with my cat close by.

The strange night noises of my new home kept me awake—a creak here, a creak there, an odd *tap, tap, tap,* the rush of water in the drains. I turned this way and that—stomach, right side, left side, back, legs curled up, legs out straight. But no matter what position I took, I couldn't relax.

Large, dark furniture, carved with vines and animal heads, crowded around me on clawed feet. It was like trying to sleep in an enchanted forest full of strange beasts. For all I knew, I'd wake in the morning and find myself far from everything I knew and loved, alone and afraid.

Finally, I got out of bed and went looking for Dad. I needed some comforting. Tink followed me, probably hoping it was time for breakfast.

I was halfway down the steps when I heard Dad say, "I can't wait to introduce you to Jen. She's a lovely girl, Moura, sweet and quiet, a little shy. Very bright."

I stopped and gripped the railing. A cold breeze blew up the stairs, but I didn't move. Dad was talking on the phone, telling a stranger about me. "She still misses her mother," he said. "It was hard for her to leave our old house, but I think the change will do her good. Maybe she'll be happier here."

He paused to give "Moura" a turn to speak and then said, "I do my best, but Jen's almost thirteen. She needs mothering, a woman to talk to her about things."

I wanted to run down the steps and yank the phone out of Dad's hand. He had no right to tell a stranger how I felt or what I needed. It was none of her business. But, angry as I was, I didn't want Dad to know I'd been eavesdropping.

"Come tomorrow afternoon," Dad said. "I'd love to give you a complete tour of the house and its furnishings. You're bound to find something perfect for your shop."

Another pause, and then Dad said, "Don't worry about a thing, Moura. Jen will absolutely adore you."

Before Dad hung up, I crept back to bed. Who was this Moura? How had my father met her? And why had he said I'd adore her? I wouldn't—I was sure of it. And I certainly wasn't going to talk to her in some mother-daughter way. Dad was the only person I needed.

Tink snuggled closer, butting his head against me, demanding to be petted. "Moura," I whispered. "I don't even like her name."

Tink rubbed his face against mine and purred even louder. That meant he agreed. He didn't like Moura, either.

I fell asleep hoping I could keep Dad away from this Moura person.

3

AT BREAKFAST, DAD was so distracted he poured orange juice on his cereal. Under different circumstances, I would have laughed and teased him, but I was still angry about what I'd overheard him tell the mysterious Moura.

"That was dumb," I muttered.

Dad laughed. "To tell you the truth, I'm a little flustered," he said. "When I came to town last month to settle Uncle Thaddeus's estate, the lawyer suggested I hire an antique dealer to assess my uncle's belongings—the furniture, the art, the bric-a-brac he once feared I'd break. He recommended a woman named Moura Winters. She runs the Dark Side of the Moon, a pricey little shop in Mingo. She's coming at one to look at the place."

I toyed with my cereal, pushing the flakes this way and that. "Were you talking to her last night?"

"Why, yes," he began, "but how—"

I shoved my cereal bowl aside, no longer hungry. "Why did you tell her about me? It's none of her business how I feel."

Dad stared at me, surprised. "Were you eavesdropping, Jen?"

"No. I was coming downstairs because I couldn't sleep,

and I heard you telling some stranger that I missed my mother, that I was lonely, that I needed a woman to talk to. You made me sound absolutely pitiful, some sad girl with no one to talk to."

Dad ran a hand through his hair. "I didn't mean to make you sound pitiful. It's just that Moura and I . . . we . . . she and I . . . well, we —"

"You and Moura what?" I gripped the edge of the table. "How long have you known her, anyway?"

"The lawyer I mentioned before introduced us," he said. "Whenever I came down to work on the house, I took Moura to dinner, a movie. . . . She's very nice, Jen. A good businesswoman, too. She knows her antiques. You'll like her, I'm sure of it. Just give her—"

I didn't wait for him to finish. With Tink bounding ahead, I ran upstairs to my room and slammed the door. Now I understood the many trips Dad had made to Great-Uncle Thaddeus's house before we moved. A plumber to see. An electrician, a carpenter, a lawyer. While I'd spent weekend after boring weekend with a babysitter, Dad had been spending time in Mingo with Moura.

When Dad knocked on my door, I told him to go away. I'd stay in my room all day if I felt like it. He was a traitor, a cheat, a liar.

"For heaven's sake," Dad protested. "Why shouldn't Moura and I—"

"Leave me alone," I said. "I don't want to hear that name again!"

After a while, Dad gave up and went downstairs. I waited a few minutes, maybe ten, maybe fifteen, and then tiptoed to his room. I found the key to the tower, neatly labeled, in the top drawer of his bureau. If I hadn't been so angry with him, I probably would have felt guilty about disobeying him, but I dropped the key into the pocket of my shorts with only a twinge of conscience.

I crept downstairs and peeked into the kitchen. Dad was lying on the floor, his head under the sink, trying to repair a leaking pipe he'd discovered.

With Tink at my heels, I slipped out the front door, circled around the house to the rear, and ran down the hill to the tower. Hidden behind the screen of overgrown bushes, I shoved the key into the padlock and turned it. It took all my strength, but at last the lock moved, and I pushed the heavy door open.

Tink and I hesitated on the threshold. The air was hot and still and thick with dust. It smelled of mold, mouse droppings, pigeon poop, and other nose-wrinkling, indefinable things. Tink scooted up the winding wooden staircase, and I followed slowly, avoiding the bones of a bird scattered on the stairs, testing each step to see if it was rotten. The wood seemed sound to me. Dad must have exaggerated to discourage me from what I was doing now.

At the top, the stairs opened into a big round room. Dim light shone through the ivy covering the small windows, giving the room a greenish tint, almost as if it were under water. A pair of pigeons, heads tucked under their wings, slept on the rafters. Mice scurried through stacks of paper and crooked piles of old books. I saw a chair here, a table there, busts of ancient Greeks and Romans, trunks and boxes, all coated with dirt and cobwebs.

I opened a few of the books, hoping to find a good story, but the mildewed pages were covered with odd symbols and marks. Runes, I thought, like the ones carved on the tower's door.

Tossing the unreadable books aside, I spied an easel standing by one of the small leaf-choked windows. A palette of dried oils sat on a table, its colors so caked with dust that it was impossible to tell what they'd once been. On the easel was a painting of a girl's face partly hidden by shadows. Her strange slanted eyes stared into mine, half afraid, half curious. Moonlight shone through the foliage and tinted her pale skin green. She was so real, I almost expected her to move or speak.

But what she'd say, I couldn't guess. She didn't look quite human.

While Tink explored the room, I looked through a stack of paintings leaning against the easel. The same girl's face stared out from two of them. In one especially eerie painting, she seemed to be trapped behind a glass wall, pressing her hands against it, as if she were desperate to escape. I had a feeling Great-Uncle Thaddeus had been trying to paint something very real to him but he hadn't gotten it right somehow.

The other paintings were of strange moonlit forests, dark

lakes, rushing rivers, caverns. In some, menacing figures peered from shadowy places. They were barely visible, and as inhuman as the girl.

I let the canvases fall back, raising a cloud of dust that made me sneeze.

Still hoping to discover a gold chalice, a ruby diadem, or, at the very least, a pile of silver coins, I took another look around the room. That's when I saw the small glass globe. Revolving slowly in the lazy summer air, it hung at the end of a tarnished silver chain suspended from a hook high above my head. Like everything else in the tower, it was filthy, but under the dirt, I was able to make out a faint spiral pattern of colors. Cleaned up, it would look pretty hanging in my bedroom window.

While Tink watched, I climbed on top of a table and reached for the globe. But, stretch as tall as I could, it was still beyond my grasp. I gathered an armload of the thickest books I could find, piled them on the table, and climbed on top. Just as my fingers brushed the globe, the books slid out from under me, and I almost fell. Startled by the commotion, mice scurried about madly and the pigeons flew out a broken window, their wings clapping like sheets of metal.

Unfazed by the ruckus, Tink stared steadily at the globe, his ears pricked, his tail twitching.

Determined to get the globe, I grabbed a rickety old chair and hefted it onto the table. After making sure it was strong enough to hold me, I stood on the seat and tried again to reach the globe. Grabbing it at last, I climbed down carefully and wiped the glass with the bottom of my T-shirt. I turned the globe this way and that, admiring its spiraling pattern of green, blue, purple, and gold. Where all the colors converged, I discovered a little spout, tightly stoppered with a cork. The glassblower must have put it there for some reason, but I had no idea why.

Tink rose on his hind legs and sniffed the globe. Dropping down on all four paws, he shivered and clicked his teeth as if he saw a mouse. But his eyes were on the globe.

"What's so interesting?" I asked him.

He mewed and reared up to reach for the globe.

"Don't," I said. "You'll break it."

I hid the globe under my shirt and hurried down the narrow steps. It was later than I thought, and I was worried Dad would call me for lunch. Shoving the tower door shut, I tried to relock the padlock, but as I fumbled with it, the rusty old thing fell apart in my fingers. Not knowing what else to do, I left the padlock on the ground and sneaked out of the bushes. With Tink bounding ahead, I ran across the lawn, hoping with every step that Dad wouldn't look out the window and see me.

In a few seconds, I was safe on the terrace behind the house, peering through the screen door. Dad was still working under the sink. He didn't see Tink or me sneak past him and tiptoe upstairs.

Leaving Tink in the hall, I locked the bathroom door and scrubbed the globe till it sparkled. When I held it up to the window, the sun shone through its rainbow of colors, casting a reflection on the floor—pale green, blue, gold, and violet shadows as delicate as moonlight.

Later I'd tell Dad I found the globe in one of the empty rooms. Or up in the attic. Or down in the basement. But for now I decided to keep it a secret.

Tink was waiting when I opened the bathroom door. Eyes fixed on the globe, he followed me to my room and watched me hide it behind a stack of games on a shelf in my closet.

"You stay away from this," I whispered to the cat. "It's not a toy for you to bat around the floor."

Tink clicked his teeth again and lashed his tail.

I shut the closet door just as Dad called, "Jen, how about giving me a hand with lunch?"

Not long after we finished our grilled-cheese sandwiches, the doorbell rang. Dad got to his feet quickly, his face flushed. "That must be Moura," he said. "Please be polite, Jen. She's our guest."

I followed him to the door, more curious than I cared to admit. A tall, slender woman stood on the porch, her narrow face paler than the moon on a December night. Her long hair was black, parted in the middle, and touched here and there with strands of silver. The frames of her tinted glasses slanted up at the ends, cat's-eye style. She wore a silky white blouse under a crimson vest, a long, swirly black skirt, and high-heeled sandals. Around her neck was a deep red stone pendant on a delicate silver chain. Matching earrings swayed when she moved her head. Her long nails were polished scarlet, and her lipstick was scarlet, too. Her fingers sparkled with rings.

I stared at Moura, fascinated by her stylish clothes and sophistication. I had to admit she was beautiful, but there was something indefinably scary about her. Moving closer to Dad, I reached for his hand and held it tight.

Moura had parked close to the house. Her car was black and low slung, as sleek as a racer. In the passenger seat was a slim black dog, just as elegant as his mistress. Expensive, I thought. And possibly dangerous. Most likely an enemy of cats.

"Hello, Hugh," Moura said, smiling at Dad. "I hope I'm not too early, but business was slow today." Her voice was low and husky, tinged with an accent of some sort—not exactly British, not exactly Irish or Scottish, but a little like all three.

"We've just finished lunch. Please come in." Dad stood back to let her enter. I'd never seen him so happy to see someone.

Moura's skirt rustled as she followed Dad into the living room and settled herself in an armchair. I expected her to remove her glasses, but she kept them on.

Dad took a seat on the sofa opposite her and beckoned to me. "Moura, I'd like you to meet my daughter, Jen," he said.

Remembering my manners, I crossed the room and shook hands with the woman. "Pleased to meet you, Miss Winters." I forced a smile to show her I was definitely not in need of mothering—especially from her.

"The pleasure is mine." Moura bared perfect teeth in a perfect smile. Her voice was soft and low, but the hand holding mine was as cold as her name. Releasing me, she added, "I've heard so much about you, Jen."

I blushed, knowing exactly what she'd heard. "Oh, you can't believe everything Dad says," I told her.

"I hope you'll visit me in my shop," Moura went on. "The Dark Side of the Moon, it's called. I have a fine collection of antique dolls. But perhaps you're too old for such things." She sighed and glanced at Dad. "Girls grow up so fast these days."

Did Moura think I was too grown-up? Tall, skinny me in my T-shirt and shorts? Most people thought I was younger than twelve. Ten, maybe. Coming from someone else, I might have felt complimented by her words, but Moura spoke as if growing up too fast was one of the evils of modern times. So I shrugged and toyed with my ponytail.

"Is that your dog in the car?" I asked.

Moura smiled. "His name is Cadoc. Do you know what that means?"

I shook my head. "It has an interesting sound," I ventured, but scary was more like it.

"In the Welsh language it means warrior. And that's what Cadoc is. My warrior, my protector."

"Warrior," I echoed, smiling stiffly. But I couldn't help wondering why Moura needed a warrior to protect her. She certainly didn't appear to be a helpless woman.

"Do you know the Welsh legends?" Dad asked her.

"Oh, yes," Moura purred. "I've read every version of *The*

Mabinogion I can find. The stories are laden with romance and magic and mystery. Ancient, yet modern. Full of meaning."

"I love *The Mabinogion* myself," Dad said. "It isn't often I meet someone who's even heard of it." He looked as pleased as if she'd given him a present. "The longer I know you, the more you surprise me. It's amazing how much we have in common."

If I hadn't been there, I was sure he would have kissed her. Instead, he contented himself by gazing at her like a teenager in love.

In the silence, Moura's eyes roamed the room, taking in Great-Uncle Thaddeus's possessions, assessing them, assessing Dad, assessing me.

"Would you like to examine my great-uncle's things now?" Dad asked, apparently not noticing Moura already had.

"Yes, of course," she murmured, "if it's convenient, Hugh."

I followed them from room to room, watching them pore over paintings, old books, furniture, glassware, china, and silver. How she saw anything through those dark glasses was a mystery worthy of *The Mabinogion*—whatever that was.

Finally, bored beyond belief, I went to my room to read. Tink opened one sleepy eye when I flopped down beside him on the bed.

I opened *The Woman in White*, an old-fashioned mystery I'd found in Great-Uncle Thaddeus's library, but I couldn't concentrate on the story. Not with Moura downstairs with my father. I kept thinking of the expression on his face when the doorbell rang, the way he'd leapt up to let her in, his flushed face, the look in his eyes.

He couldn't really be in love with her, not Dad. Unlike some of my friends' divorced fathers, he'd never shown the least interest in finding a girlfriend. He was a nice-looking man, tall and lanky, with a full brown beard, but his hair was thinning and he had no style. Today he was wearing an old navy polo shirt so faded it was almost gray. His jeans were white at the knees, the seams frayed, and they hung loosely on him.

Even if Dad were in love with Moura, why would she love him? Moura, owner of Cadoc, the warrior dog; Moura, with her perfect black hair and her beautiful clothes; Moura, with her sleek black sporty car; Moura, with her chilling eyes and smile. Moura, who made me feel uncomfortable, ugly, and dull.

Yet with all her glamour, she seemed to return Dad's interest. Did she think my father was rich? Was she after the house and its contents? Who knew what Moura wanted? Great-Uncle Thaddeus's antiques? Dad's heart? Maybe both.

I shouldn't have left my father alone with her. Tossing my book aside, I ran downstairs, fearful of what Moura might have said or done in my absence.

I FOUND THEM IN the kitchen having tea and talking softly.

"How did you ever end up in a boring little town in the mountains of West Virginia?" Dad was asking Moura.

She smiled. "It's a long story, Hugh."

Dad reached for her hand. "I love long stories."

When I cleared my throat loudly, Moura looked at me. She'd finally removed her glasses. They lay on the table beside her cup, casting colored shadows on the tablecloth. Her eyes were large and a light greenish gray, the pupils ringed with yellow.

"Have a seat, Jen." Moura motioned toward a chair. Her lips curved briefly into a smile that didn't reach her strange eyes. Somehow she made me feel unwelcome without being anything but polite.

Reluctantly, I slid into the seat and sat there tongue-tied with discomfort, the third person, totally unnecessary. Dad patted my hand, but I had a feeling he wished I hadn't interrupted the conversation.

Cadoc lay at Moura's feet, his head resting on her sandals.

When he saw me, he raised his head and stared with eyes as pale and cold as his mistress's. Although he didn't growl, I moved my chair away, ready to run if he so much as opened his mouth. I was glad Tink hadn't followed me downstairs.

Moura patted the dog's head. "Cadoc won't hurt you, Jen," she said. "Come closer."

Feeling childish, I forced myself to do as she said. Her perfume was strong, cloying. It made my head ache just to sit near her. And her eyes . . . When she looked at me, I wished she'd kept her glasses on.

"Cadoc," Moura said, "this is Jen."

The dog sat up and extended a paw for me to shake. I took it gingerly, feeling the hard claws housed in soft fur and velvety footpads. "Pleased to meet you," I lied.

The introduction finished, I backed away from Moura and her dog, relishing the distance from both of them.

"Isn't he amazing?" Dad asked me. "Moura has trained that dog perfectly."

I nodded, but I was glad to see Cadoc lie down again.

"Perhaps we could take a walk with Cadoc one fine day," Moura suggested to me. "I know a lovely path by the river."

Dad went on for a while about how much fun it would be to ramble through the woods with the scariest dog I'd ever seen. Of course, he didn't think Cadoc was scary. No, he was Moura's dog and just as perfect as she was.

During a lull in the conversation, I asked Moura what she thought of Great-Uncle Thaddeus's things.

She smiled. "The house is full of treasures—paintings, sculpture, porcelain, silver, old books. If your father wants to sell his great-uncle's possessions, he'll be a rich man indeed. Why, the dining-room furniture alone is worth at least fifteen thousand dollars."

I stared at her, absolutely amazed. "Who on earth would pay that much for old furniture?"

"Collectors," Moura said, "dealers, maybe even a museum. The set is solid walnut, handcrafted, and in perfect condition."

I turned to Dad. "Are you going to sell it?"

He shrugged. "Maybe, maybe not. We just moved in, Jen. I want to live with Uncle Thaddeus's things for a while before I make any decisions."

When Dad paused to sip his tea, Moura turned to me, her eyes keen. "I was expecting to find something I was told your uncle owned," she said slowly, "but I didn't see it anywhere."

"What were you looking for?" I asked.

"A glass globe, about this big." Moura cupped her hands to show me. "It's decorated with a swirling pattern of colors. There's a little spout on one side and a loop at the top so it can be hung in a window."

While Moura described my globe, I drank my tea silently. I didn't dare look at my father for fear I'd give myself away. The globe was mine. I'd found it, and I wasn't going to give it to anyone—especially Moura.

"Some people call it a sun catcher," Moura went on, "but its original name was witch catcher. In the old days, superstitious people believed the pretty pattern in the glass had the power to draw witches and other evil creatures through the spout and into the globe. Trapped inside, the witch was powerless."

"Is that right?" Dad leaned toward Moura, amused by her story.

More worried than amused, I studied the tea leaves in my cup, wishing I could tell my own fortune. I was haunted by the girl I'd seen in the painting, her hands pressed against what I'd thought was a glass wall. Had Great-Uncle Thaddeus captured a witch in that globe? Was she at this very moment hidden in my closet?

Moura smiled her strange smile. "Well, it's certainly true that the globes were called witch catchers, and people hung them in their windows to protect themselves." She stared for a moment into her own teacup, her long slender fingers curved around the fragile china. "Today witch catchers are valued for their beauty, but I find their history fascinating. Suppose the old superstitions are true and witches actually are held captive in those pretty globes? Suppose you broke one and the witch escaped?"

As she spoke, Moura gazed directly at me. Her voice was light, even playful, but the expression in her eyes was anything but humorous.

I shrugged and looked away. If Moura thought she could scare me into confessing I had the trap, she was mistaken.

"Nonsense," Dad said with a laugh. "These days, you

won't find witches roaming the countryside just waiting to be trapped in glass globes."

"You'd be surprised," Moura said in a voice so low Dad didn't seem to hear. But I did. Maybe because she was looking at me, not my father. Despite myself, I shivered. Was she warning me? Or just trying to scare me?

"I have a client who collects witch catchers," Moura went on in a normal voice. "He's most anxious to acquire another. I know for a fact he's willing to pay several hundred dollars for the one your uncle owned."

Her head swung toward me, and her long hair swirled around her pale face. "Have you seen the globe, Jen?"

Taken by surprise, I shook my head. Near my feet Cadoc stirred and sighed, his breath warm on my leg.

"We haven't explored the tower," Dad said. "Maybe Uncle Thaddeus kept it up there."

"There's nothing in the tower," I said. "You told me so yourself."

"Would you mind if I had a look?" Moura asked.

"We'll all go," Dad said. "Jen's dying to explore the place."

"But you told me it's not safe," I reminded him. "You said it was about to fall down."

Dad laughed. "Goodness, Jen, I didn't think you believed anything I told you."

He meant it as a joke, but his words stung. Sarcasm wasn't Dad's style.

"I'm sure the tower's perfectly safe," Moura said, apparently missing both the joke and the sarcasm. Getting to her feet, she reached for her glasses.

Reluctantly, I followed Dad and Moura outside. Cadoc ran gracefully ahead, his long, lithe body stretching as if his bones were strung together with elastic.

The first thing Dad noticed, of course, was the broken lock. He turned to me and frowned. "Do you know anything about this, Jen?"

"A burglar could have done it last night," I said, choosing my words carefully. Not a lie, but not quite the truth, either.

Dad stared at me, his eyes filled with suspicion. "What thief would come all the way out here just to break into this old ruin?"

Moura surprised me by saying, "Jen may be right, Hugh. We've had several robberies lately. Probably teenagers with nothing else to do."

Dad obviously didn't want to argue with Moura, but I could tell he wasn't convinced I was being truthful. Without saying more, he shoved the door open, letting out a whiff of dank, moldy air. Moura stepped back, her nose wrinkled in distaste.

Dad smiled. "The tower's been closed for so long, it's no wonder it smells bad. Once we get to the top, you won't notice the odor."

When Moura hesitated, Dad took her arm. "Come on, Moura. Where's your sense of adventure?"

Cadoc ran up the winding stairs, ahead of us all. Moura

allowed Dad to lead her across the threshold and up the creaky old stairs, but the expression of distaste stayed on her face.

Unfortunately, I hadn't thought to straighten up before I'd left. The chair stood on the table where I'd put it. Worse yet, the dust was marked with footprints, clearly showing the ridges on the soles of my running shoes.

Dad frowned at me. "Someone's been up here," he said. "With feet just about the size of yours. How do you explain that, Jen?"

Moura surprised me again by laughing. "Children will be children," she told Dad. "They're as curious as cats. And just as devious."

"Let's hope they have nine lives as well." Dad gave me a look that plainly said I'd hear more about this later.

Pretending indifference, I watched the two of them search the room. Dad bumped his head on a low rafter. Moura coughed. A pigeon took wing from a rafter and flew out a broken window. Mice scurried from one hiding place to another. Cadoc made no move to chase them. He seemed more interested in prowling about, sniffing at things.

When they'd looked in all the obvious places, Dad turned his attention to his great-uncle's paintings, but Moura came to me. "You're sure you didn't see the witch catcher, Jen? It might have been hanging in one of the windows."

I gave Moura the sweet look that worked so well with my teachers. "I didn't stay up here very long. The dust bothered me." As proof, I covered my mouth and coughed.

"But why is the chair on the table?" Moura asked. "Was there something up there that you were trying to reach?"

I shrugged. "I wanted to see out the window better."

Moura continued to study me, her eyes hidden behind those tinted glasses. No trace of her earlier smile lingered on her lips.

I drew away, not wanting her to see how uncomfortable she'd made me. Somehow she knew I had the glass globe. Not guessed. *Knew.* And it scared me.

With a sigh, Moura touched Dad's arm. "I think we've seen all there is to see up here," she said.

"Before we go, take a look at these," Dad said. "They remind me of those strange old Victorian paintings of fairies."

An odd look crossed Moura's face, but it was gone before Dad saw it. "Oh, yes," she said quickly. "Do you realize that most of the artists were lunatics? Some were incarcerated in insane asylums." She laughed. "That's where believing in fairies leads—straight to Bedlam."

Dad nodded, too absorbed in the paintings to hear the tension in her voice and laugh.

Her face half in shadow, Moura turned to me. "According to legend, fairies aren't the dear little creatures you imagine them to be. On the contrary, they are malicious, spiteful, and completely untrustworthy."

Her soft voice concealed a warning meant for me. Danger tingled in the very air around us. But danger from what? Fairies? The globe hidden in my closet? I drew closer to my father, comforted by his everyday ordinariness.

Pointing to the painting on the easel, Dad said, "This girl certainly has an unearthly quality. Is she good or evil?"

"Wicked beyond imagining." A flash of hatred crossed Moura's face—gone, of course, before Dad noticed. "Look at her eyes, the curious slant, the malice in their depths. She's a fairy I wouldn't want to meet in a dark wood."

"How about you, Jen?" Dad asked. "What do you think? I can't quite make up my mind about her."

"She looks scared," I whispered. "Not evil."

Moura removed her glasses and contemplated me, her head tilted so that her hair fell straight and shiny to one side. "Children," she murmured. "So naive, so unaware of danger. They truly need to be protected from themselves."

Unnerved by her disdainful gaze, I took a step backward and almost stumbled over Cadoc. He raised his head and growled softly, as if he, too, were warning me. I didn't know which one scared me more—the hound or his mistress.

With a smile, Moura turned back to Dad. "The same client who collects witch traps has a keen interest in fairy lore. Shall I tell him about these paintings? He'd be willing to pay a great deal for them."

Dad hesitated before he answered. "I'm not sure I want to part with them just yet," he said at last. "But if your client wants to look at them, I have no objection."

Taking the paintings with him, Dad led the way downstairs with Moura behind him, her long skirt flowing. Cadoc followed, close at her heels. I brought up the rear, allowing plenty of distance between myself and the dog.

At the bottom of the steps, I lingered in the tower doorway and watched Dad and Moura walk across the lawn, their heads close, talking softly. Cadoc loped in circles around them, as lean and graceful as a greyhound but far more menacing.

When I caught up with them, I heard Moura tell Dad, "I'm sorry I can't accept your invitation. I have a business engagement this evening. Perhaps tomorrow night?"

Dad's face brightened. "That will be even better. I'll have more time to plan a great dinner for you."

Moura waved to Dad and me and got into her car. Cadoc made himself comfortable in the passenger seat, and off they went, leaving a cloud of dust behind.

As soon as the car was out-of-sight, Dad turned to me.

"I'm disappointed in you, Jen," he said. "Not only did you go into the tower, but you lied about it. Worse yet, I have a feeling you know exactly where that witch catcher is."

Ashamed to meet his eyes, I looked at the ground and shook my head. Even though it upset me to lie to my father, I had no intention of giving the glass globe to Moura. I enjoyed knowing I had something she wanted.

That night, I retrieved the globe from its hiding place and stared into the glass. I saw nothing. No witch. No evil spirit. It was all nonsense anyway. How could a full-size witch be sucked into a glass globe no bigger than a softball?

I strung a green ribbon through the loop at the top and tied the ribbon around my curtain rod. The globe spun slowly in the night breeze, catching light from the moon.

Tink watched the globe turn, his eyes big. He rose on his hind legs as if he longed to bat it back and forth like one of his toys.

"Oh, no, you don't." I scooped him up, and he snuggled against me purring, his eyes fixed on the globe.

The breeze blew harder, and the globe spun faster, casting its pattern of delicate blues and greens and violets faintly on the moonlit floor. An insect buzzed loudly—a cicada hidden in the ivy draping my window, I guessed.

Suddenly, Tink twisted out of my arms and leapt at the globe as if he meant to knock it down.

"No!" I shouted and gave him a light spank on his side. He hissed at me and ran under the bed.

I knelt down and peered at him, almost invisible in the shadows. "I'm sorry, Tink," I whispered. "I was afraid you'd break it—and let the witch out."

I was joking, but he growled at me, his tail twice as big as usual.

"Tink!" I reached for him, but he growled again, louder this time. "What's the matter with you? Are you afraid of that cicada?"

I reached for him again but got the same grumpy response. "Okay, stay there. See if I care, silly old cat."

I slid under the covers and turned out the bedside lamp. The cicada cried louder, buzzing as if it were in my room, not in the ivy outside the window.

Drowsily, I watched the witch catcher turn this way and that, subject to every whim of the breeze. The glass seemed to glow with a greenish light, as if it caught moonlight as well as sunlight. A moon catcher, I thought, liking that better than witch catcher.

Slowly I slid into a deep sleep full of strange dreams. In the first, I was alone in a dark forest. Tall trees loomed over me, hiding the sky. There was no movement, no sound; not one leaf stirred, yet I sensed someone watching me. I turned slowly, fearfully, but saw nothing. I walked farther. The mossy ground was soft and damp. My feet sank into it, making no noise but releasing the smell of decaying leaves. I was frightened. I tried to run, but the soft ground held me back.

Suddenly, not very far ahead, Moura stepped out from behind a tree, her face like the moon, her clothes like the night, her glasses trapping darkness. "Give me the witch catcher, Jen," she said in her soft voice. "I know you have it."

I looked at my cupped hands. Though I hadn't noticed it earlier, I was holding the globe. An odd green light seeped through my fingers, and the glass warmed my skin.

Moura came closer, taller and more menacing with each step. Her neck lengthened, her body thinned. A black gown clung to her body in a scaly pattern. "No games," she whispered. "You don't know who I really am. You don't know what I can do. Foolish girl, you don't even know what you hold in your hands."

I tried to call for help but could do no more than gasp. The globe grew warmer, its light shone brighter, and it moved in my hands like an egg about to break open.

"Give it to me quickly!" Moura grabbed my hands and tried to take the globe. Its heat burned her fingers, and she sprang back with a curse. Dropping to the ground, she took the shape of a long black snake.

Just as she reared to strike, the dream changed, and I was alone in the tower. The moon shone through the tiny windows, illuminating the painting of the girl's face. Suddenly, the leaves behind her stirred and rustled. Turning her strange eyes to me, she pressed her hands against the canvas as if she were trapped behind a wall. "Help me!" she cried. "Please help me."

Terrified, I backed away and tripped on something long and sinuous. The snake slithered across the tower floor behind me. But I wasn't what it wanted this time. Its attention was focused on the girl in the painting.

"Help me," the girl begged again as the snake coiled around the base of the easel.

But I could do nothing, neither move nor speak. Paralyzed, I watched the snake rise higher and strike the painting. At the same moment, a flock of crows smashed through the window, exploding into the room, filling it with wild cries, sharp beaks, and black feathers. The serpent fled, the crows swooping after it.

The girl was a painting again. The leaves were still and so was she. I was alone in the dark, silent tower.

I woke suddenly with the image of the girl's face before me. In my bedroom window, the witch catcher sparkled in the morning light. Tink perched on the windowsill beneath it, watching the globe intently, his ears pricked as if he heard something.

While the cat watched, I carried the globe back to its hiding place in my closet. Still under the spell of my dream, I almost expected it to feel warm in my hands, to glow and pulsate, but its glass surface remained cool.

5

AFTER BREAKFAST, DAD suggested a trip to Mingo. Since he'd seen Uncle Thaddeus's paintings, he had an itch to buy some art supplies and start working on his own pictures. He also had to buy food for tonight's dinner.

"There's a little ice cream parlor you might enjoy," he added.

Mingo wasn't exactly a mecca for shopping. The only store that sold art supplies was a small place called Crafty Corners. I followed Dad inside and looked at scrapbook supplies while he talked to a woman with long silvery blond hair pulled back in a careless knot. She had a nice smile, and she seemed happy to show Dad a small display of acrylic paints, drawing tablets, and brushes.

"I'm afraid we don't have much for serious artists," she said. "You might have better luck buying supplies online. That's what I do."

"Do you paint?" Dad asked.

She shrugged. "A little."

"Landscapes? People? Abstract or figurative? Oils? Watercolors? Acrylics?"

"Oh, some of everything. How about you?"

In a few moments, they were talking art. I wandered around the store looking at sheets of decals, a display of artsy rubber stamps and colored ink pads, sprays of fake flowers, and plasticine clay. Soon bored, I returned to the counter just in time to hear the woman say, "You live in the castle? The one with the tower? I've always been fascinated by that place."

"Thaddeus Mostyn was my great-uncle," Dad said. "I'm his only heir."

"Was he as strange as people say?" The woman leaned across the counter, waiting for Dad to answer.

He shrugged. "He was definitely eccentric—but brilliant."

"He painted, didn't he? Fantastical things in the style of Arthur Rackham."

"Yes. Moura Winters knows a man who collects that sort of thing. She can arrange a sale, if I'm interested."

At the mention of Moura's name, the woman drew back slightly. "The owner of the Dark Side of the Moon?"

Dad nodded. "I don't know much about antiques. Moura's been very helpful."

"I bet she has," the woman said.

I tugged Dad's sleeve. "How about that ice cream? I'm hungry."

Dad paid for a set of watercolors, a few brushes, and a tablet. "Good luck with your painting," he said to the woman.

She smiled her nice smile. "You'll have to bring your work in and show it to me sometime," she said. "The local coffee shop displays paintings. New show every month. My name's Rosie. I help choose what they hang."

Dad nodded. "Thanks, Rosie. Maybe I'll do that."

As we left, I glanced over my shoulder. Rosie smiled at me and raised her hand in a sort of wave. But it was Dad she was looking at.

The ice cream parlor turned out to be a Dairy Queen. While we were waiting for our order, I said, "That woman was flirting with you."

Dad laughed. "Don't be silly. She was just friendly, that's all."

The only grocery store in Mingo was small and dingy compared to the big suburban chains back home. I was bored in less than five minutes.

Leaving Dad to select things for dinner, I took a walk. The morning was already hot, but the streets were quiet and shady. I passed two churches, a hardware store, a beauty shop, and a video-rental store. The faded posters in its windows were from movies I'd already seen.

At the end of the block, I glimpsed a sign for the Dark Side of the Moon hanging above the door of a narrow brick house. Ready to run if I saw Moura, I ducked behind a tree across the street from the shop. Despite my dislike of the woman, I wanted to learn all I could about her. For Dad's sake, I told myself. To protect him from making a big mistake.

From my hiding place, I studied the antiques arranged

artfully in the window. Porcelain vases, crystal goblets, and ornamental figurines sat atop a dark chest. On one side was a fancy carved chair fit for a king's throne, and on the other was an ancient baby carriage holding a doll with a pretty china face. Judging by the shop's stained-glass sign and its display of perfect objects, Moura was after serious collectors, not people trying to furnish a house with cheap used furniture.

While I stood there spying, a little bell jangled and the shop's door opened. A tall, slim man stepped out. His hair was silver, and so was his neatly trimmed beard and mustache. He wore a dark suit and white shirt, a red tie knotted tightly under his collar. Altogether he made the same impression Moura made—handsome, but scary somehow.

Moura followed the man outside. Today she wore stylish black slacks and a crimson T-shirt. Despite the bright sunlight, she wasn't wearing her tinted glasses. Her hair, with its curious silver streaks, hung loose and long and straight. No matter how much time I spent blow-drying and brushing my hair, I'd never come close to achieving that sort of perfection.

There was no sign of Cadoc.

Moura and the man stood on the steps for a few minutes talking. Neither of them laughed or smiled. Moura gestured fiercely, and the man nodded, his face stern. When he turned to leave, she followed him down the sidewalk.

"Ciril," she called in that low, soft voice I detested.

He paused and waited for her. They were much closer to me now. Fearful of being seen, I flattened myself behind the tree.

"While you're viewing the paintings tomorrow," Moura said, "I'll get the trap somehow. Though she denies it, the girl has it. She's a bad liar."

The trap—it was clear Moura meant the witch catcher. Well, she wouldn't get her hands on it. And neither would that man. The witch catcher was mine. I'd found it. And I was keeping it.

"You should have searched the tower while the house was empty." Ciril spoke like a classy English actor, the kind you see in old movies—Laurence Olivier or someone like that. But distinguished as his voice sounded, it had a chilling quality.

"You know I couldn't enter," Moura said, touching his arm. "The door was sealed against me."

Ciril considered her for a moment. "Excuses, excuses." He brushed her hand from his sleeve. "You disappoint me, Moura."

"But, Ciril—"

The man tightened his grip on his briefcase. "Make the appointment for tomorrow morning at ten. I'll see you then."

He turned his back on her and strode away, his face angry. I held my breath, fearing he'd cross the street and see me, but he got into a luxurious silver car that was parked at the curb. Moura stood on the sidewalk and watched the car pull away. The expression on her face was unreadable, but certainly not happy. Turning abruptly, she retreated to her shop. The bell jangled as the door slammed shut behind her.

I stayed where I was for a few more minutes. If Moura looked out her window and saw me, she'd know I'd been eavesdropping. But what had I heard? Moura wanted the witch catcher—I already knew that. So apparently did Ciril. Badly enough to steal it.

But why had she said the door was sealed against her? What did that mean? Despite the warm sunlight, I shivered. Moura, Ciril, Cadoc, the talk of witches and evil spirits and sealed doors, the eerie paintings in the tower, the gloomy house—something strange was going on, but I had no idea what. Except that it involved the witch catcher.

When a delivery truck pulled up in front of the shop, blocking Moura's view of the street, I dashed back to the grocery store. Dad was in the parking lot, pushing his shopping cart toward our van. "Where have you been, Jen?"

"Just walking around." I gestured at the neighborhood.

"Did you see Moura's shop?"

"Yes, but I didn't go in."

"Why not? She would have been delighted to show you her doll collection."

"I outgrew dolls in fifth grade, Dad. And I never have liked antique stores. They're dark and smelly and full of dead people's stuff."

"Not Moura's shop. She has museum-quality furniture."

I shrugged. "Rich or poor, the people who owned that furniture are dead." I watched Dad unlock the van. "Besides, she had a man with her. They seemed to have a lot to say to each other."

Dad looked at me sharply. "He must have been a customer."

"I think he was more than that." I felt ashamed of myself, but I kept talking, deliberately putting doubts in Dad's head. "He was very distinguished-looking, handsome like an old-fashioned movie star. They acted like they'd known each other a long time."

Dad frowned, but all he said was, "Help me load the groceries into the van, Jen."

"You sure bought a lot of food," I said.

He smiled a little sheepishly. "I want to cook a spectacular meal for Moura," he confessed.

Dad spent most of the afternoon preparing a feast to impress Queen Moura. A salad of field greens, beef Wellington, baby carrots, rice pilaf, freshly baked bread, a bottle of red wine from Great-Uncle Thaddeus's cellar, and an amazing pie made with fresh strawberries and real whipped cream. For a while I hung around, talking and trying to help, but Dad finally shooed me away. "You know what they say about chefs," he said.

"Too many spoil the witch's brew," I whispered to myself.

I went outside and sat on the back steps. Tink looked up drowsily from his nap in the sun and purred like a furry little motor. I scratched the soft yellow fur under his chin, but my mind was on the witch catcher. Why was a pretty glass globe so important to Moura and Ciril? What was so special about it?

Dad poked his head out the door. "It's after five. Why don't you go and change for dinner, Jen?"

I stared at him. "What's wrong with what I'm wearing?"

"Nothing, normally," Dad said. "But we have a special guest tonight—that means a coat and tie for me and a dress for you."

"What's so special about Moura Winters?" I should have stopped with that, but I went on to say, "I don't even like her, if you want to know the truth."

Dad looked hurt. "I don't understand you, Jen. Moura's a fine, intelligent woman—just the sort to take an interest in you and give you some guidance."

"She's the last person on earth I'd turn to for guidance." I scooped up Tink and got to my feet. Once I'd said I didn't like Moura, the rest of my thoughts came tumbling out. "As far as I can tell, all that woman wants are Great-Uncle Thaddeus's things. Once she makes a bundle selling them to some rich client, you'll never see Moura Winters again."

Dad grabbed my arm to keep me from running past him. "That's a terrible thing to say, Jen, and completely unfounded."

"When I was near her shop this morning," I said, "I heard her tell that man about the witch catcher. He said she should have taken it before we moved in, and she said she would have but the tower was sealed against her."

Dad looked puzzled. "That makes absolutely no sense, Jen. You must have misunderstood." He leaned closer to study my face. "Were you spying on Moura?"

"I just happened to see her and the man talking," I said. "Ciril—that's his name. They didn't see me, and I didn't think I should interrupt them, so—"

"So you eavesdropped again." He shook his head crossly. "This is real life, Jen, not a Nancy Drew mystery. I thought you outgrew playing detective around the same time you outgrew dolls."

My face flushed red-hot. It was true. When we were ten, my friends and I had read a zillion Nancy Drew books and then spent a whole summer spying on our neighbors in hopes of solving a mystery, like our favorite girl detective. Maybe Mr. Eliot had a counterfeit money press in his garage, perhaps Mrs. Miller kept a kidnapped baby in the basement, possibly Mr. Palestro robbed banks, and so on. The trouble was, we never proved any of these things. School started, and we eventually forgot our detective game.

"This is different," I protested. "I heard Moura say she'd get the witch catcher—even if I had it."

Dad gave me a disgusted look. "That's enough, Jen. Go upstairs and put on a dress. Moura will be here in less than an hour."

"Don't say I didn't warn you about her," I muttered.

Safe in my room, I opened the closet door and peeked behind the stack of boxes. The witch catcher lay where I'd left it, in a nest of old sweatshirts. Carefully, I heaped a few T-shirts on top of it and pushed the whole pile farther back into the darkest corner.

Sure that Moura would never find the globe, I pulled my one and only dress off a hanger and shut the closet door. I shed my shorts and T-shirt and dropped the dress over my head. Just as I feared, I'd grown since fifth-grade graduation. The flowered cotton looked hopelessly out-of-date. The waist was too high and the skirt too short. In my opinion, I'd looked much better in the clothes lying on the floor, but I supposed Dad would send me up to change again if I went down in anything but a dress. What did it matter how I looked, anyway? I didn't care what Moura thought about me.

While I combed my hair, I heard Dad come upstairs, whistling. It pained me to hear how happy he sounded. If only I could convince him Moura was unworthy of his love.

But I had an awful feeling it was too late. I'd tried to warn him about Moura and Ciril and their plans to get the witch catcher. And what had happened? Instead of believing me, his own daughter, he'd accused me of spying and playing Nancy Drew detective games, as if I were still ten years old.

Well, Dad would learn the truth about Moura someday. He'd be sorry then that he hadn't listened to me.

6

AT SIX O'CLOCK, the doorbell rang. Moura was punctual, I had to say that much for her. And alone. The dreadful Cadoc must have been left in town to protect the Dark Side of the Moon.

Dad seated Moura in the living room for a drink before dinner. While they sipped their wine, I watched her. As usual, she wore red and black, a sleeveless dress this time with skinny shoulder straps and a long skirt, made from a gauzy black and red print fabric. Around her neck was the same pendant she'd worn before.

Moura turned to me with a smile. "What a sweet little dress, Jen. You look adorable."

I sipped my ginger ale and stared at the floor. What twelve-year-old girl wants to look adorable? It was enough to make me throw up. Plus I knew she didn't mean a word of it. She was just trying to make a good impression on my father by showing him she cared about me.

Dad tapped my knee. "Jen, Moura just paid you a compliment. What do you say?"

"Thanks," I muttered, without looking at her or Dad. Did they both have to speak to me as if I were a little kid?

"Jen's always been shy," Dad apologized to Moura. He might just as well have said I was subnormal.

"Ah, well," Moura said as if I were of no importance anyway. "I must tell you, Hugh, that my client, Ciril Ashbourne, is anxious to see the paintings and some of the furniture. Would it be convenient for me to bring him here tomorrow at ten?"

At the mention of Ciril Ashbourne's name, Dad shot me a look as if to say, "There, didn't I tell you? You saw Moura with a client, not a rival."

To Moura, Dad said, "Of course. I'd be happy to show him the paintings." He offered Moura more wine, but she shook her head.

"One glass is my limit." She smiled. "I have to drive, you know."

The conversation meandered on, taking one boring turn after another. They talked about the advantages of living in the country compared with those of the city. Better air, low crime, no rush-hour traffic in the country, but no good restaurants, no theater, no decent libraries, and so on. When they'd beaten that subject to death, they moved to politics. Here Dad did most of the talking. While he aired his views on the importance of the environment, gun control, and free speech, Moura said nothing. She just smiled and nodded from time to time as if she agreed with his liberal views. I was tempted to ask her a question to see if she'd listened to a word Dad had said, but I was in enough trouble already.

At last it was time to move to the dining room. Moura

looked suitably impressed by the fresh flowers Dad had bought for a centerpiece. I lit the candles, and she admired the silver Dad had made me polish.

"Kirk Repoussé," she said admiringly, running her long nails over the knife handle's delicate floral pattern. "While your great-uncle's parents were alive, this house was the scene of marvelous dinner parties, Hugh. Couples arrived in carriages. The women wore long, shimmering gowns with bustles, and the men dressed in tails. So formal. So elegant. Dancing in the ballroom, the rooms lit by candles in crystal chandeliers—" She broke off to take a sip of water.

"I suppose you remember it all," I said sarcastically, earning a frown from Dad.

"Of course not," Moura replied, her voice as pleasant as ever. "My grandmother used to tell me stories about this house. She was the Mostyns' maid when she was no older than you, Jen. In those days, children often went into service at the age of twelve."

She smiled at me, but her pale eyes were humorless. No doubt she wished she could get rid of me that easily. "Aren't you the lucky one?" she said in that low voice of hers. "Nothing to do all day but explore this fascinating old place. Why, there's no telling what a bright-eyed girl might find tucked away somewhere."

"No," I said, returning her bright, empty smile. "There's just no telling."

Dad began serving the beef Wellington, and the subject

changed to the meal, which was indeed delicious. If Dad could win Moura by feeding her, he would soon have her heart. If she had one, that is.

By the time we'd eaten the strawberry pie, my too-small dress felt even smaller and tighter. I would have liked to steal away to my room, change into comfortable clothes, and read till I fell asleep, but I'd promised Dad I'd clean up. Feeling like Moura's grandmother the housemaid, I cleared the table and began washing the dishes.

While I slaved at the sink, Dad and Moura returned to the living room to finish off dinner with coffee and liqueur served in teeny glasses. Every now and then I heard Dad laugh.

As soon as I finished the dishes, I tiptoed down the hall and stood in the shadows outside the living room door. Once you acquire detective skills, you never lose them.

"I'm afraid Jen doesn't care for me," Moura said, as if this were a great sorrow to her.

Dad sighed. "She's had me all to herself since she was two years old," he said slowly. "It's hard for her to share me, I guess."

"Yes," Moura said, "I thought that might be it. I suppose I'll have to win her over somehow. Perhaps if I spent more time with her. Just the two of us. Maybe I could take her shopping in Charles Town."

"That's a wonderful idea," Dad said. "Jen used to go shopping with her friends' mothers, but now they're a day's drive from here. When school starts in the fall, she'll make new friends, but until then she's on her own with nobody but the cat and me for company."

I grimaced. There was Dad, up to his old tricks, thinking he knew what I wanted, when I couldn't imagine anything worse than spending a day shopping with Moura.

"Jen has a secretive side, doesn't she?" Moura went on. "I'm positive she knows exactly where that witch catcher is, but for some reason she won't admit it."

"Why does it matter so much?" Dad asked. "You say the house is full of valuable things, from furniture to books. If the witch catcher makes Jen happy, why shouldn't she keep it? Not that I think she has it, of course."

"Good for you, Dad," I whispered.

Moura touched Dad's knee and leaned closer to him. "It's a very rare and unusual piece, Hugh. If it means so much to Jen, I'm sure I can find another one just as pretty, but not as valuable."

She gazed at Dad, her lips parted, and he murmured her name. The next moment they were embracing. I drew back, too upset to watch, and tiptoed upstairs to my room. Tink was asleep on my bed, and I lay down beside him.

"What am I going to do?" I whispered to the cat. "He's falling in love with her. Suppose he marries her?"

Tink looked at me as if he knew the answer to everything, but instead of telling me, he began licking his paw.

I rolled over on my back and stared at the closet door. As

soon as I heard Moura leave, I'd get the witch catcher and hang it in the window. The sight of it comforted me somehow.

I must have dozed off waiting to hear Moura's car drive away. When I woke up, Dad was leaning over me. "You fell asleep in your dress, honey," he said. "Get your pajamas on and go to bed properly."

I sat up, feeling groggy, the taste of dinner in my mouth. "Is Moura still here?"

Dad shook his head. "She left about ten minutes ago."

I glanced at my clock. "It's two a.m.," I said. "What were you doing all this time?"

Dad looked out the window and shrugged. "Talking," he said.

"About what?"

He turned to me then, his face shining. "Moura's agreed to marry me," he said. "I can't believe it. A woman like her, so beautiful, so intelligent, so charming. What can she possibly see in me?"

I flung myself back on the bed and lay flat, too shocked to say anything. Certainly not congratulations. Maybe I could manage condolences.

Dad reached down and smoothed my hair. "Be happy for me, Jen. Once you get to know her, I know you'll love her as much as I do. She's very fond of you already. In fact, she told me she's always wanted a daughter."

I turned my head to escape Dad's hand. "I'm not fond of

Moura," I muttered. "And I've never wanted to be anybody's daughter but yours."

Dad sighed. "Jen, please. I love Moura, and I hope someday soon you'll love her, too. But no matter how you feel now, I expect you to be respectful of her, to be friendly and polite, to make an effort to accept her as my wife and your stepmother."

"Just go away," I said. "And leave me alone. I don't want to talk about it anymore."

Dad got to his feet. "Moura warned me you'd be jealous," he said heavily. "But I'd hoped you might prove her wrong."

I sat up again. "I'm not jealous!" I shouted. "I just don't like her, and I don't trust her, and I think you're making a big mistake! She's mean and greedy, and she's got you completely fooled!"

"That's enough, Jen." Dad strode across my room to the door. For a second he hesitated. "I'm very disappointed in you."

With that, he walked out and shut the door behind him. I lay motionless and listened to his bedroom door close with a loud bang. It was the first time Dad had ever been truly angry with me. And it was all Moura's fault.

I must have dozed off again. The next time I opened my eyes it was almost dawn and I was still wearing my dress. The summer night was warm, and I was sweaty and uncomfortable. I undressed and hurled my clothes on the floor. Never would I wear that dumb dress again. Never. I hated it.

I put on my pajamas and lifted the witch catcher from its hiding place on the closet shelf. After I hung it in my window, I studied its delicate, swirling colors. The night was still except for the cicadas' increasingly loud buzz.

No matter what Moura said or did, the globe was mine, not hers. Great-Uncle Thaddeus had left all his belongings to my father. Moura had no right to anything in the house or the tower—not a cup, not a spoon, not even an ashtray. And certainly not the witch catcher.

AN HOUR LATER, I woke to a gray sky promising rain. After hiding the witch catcher safely away, I dressed and left the house without seeing Dad. Let him come and look for me if he wanted me. I doubted he'd miss me for hours.

Tink followed me across the lawn, bounding ahead and then waiting to see if I was coming. He often acted more like a dog than a cat, but true to his nature, he couldn't be counted on. Sometimes he was in the mood for a walk. Sometimes he wasn't. Today I was gladder than usual for his company.

Ignoring the dark clouds, I followed a narrow path that twisted downhill into the woods behind the tower. The shade was dense, the light greenish. Grapevines dangled here and there, poison ivy flourished, and the ground was cool and mossy under my bare feet. The air smelled of old leaves, wet earth, and damp, growing things. Crows squabbled and bluejays shrieked. Now and then a songbird warbled.

After a half-hour's walk, Tink and I heard the sound of water. Soon we came to a stream of dark, deep water, running fast over stones. On the bank sat seven boulders, lined up as if someone had placed them there. I climbed to the top of the biggest and looked around—nothing but trees as far as I could see. It was easy to imagine Tink and I had wandered into a magical forest, unknown to anyone but the two of us.

I looked down at my cat, who was investigating a dense growth of ferns. "We're in an enchanted place," I told him. "A unicorn could crash out of the bushes any second. We might see a dragon on the hill or find a fairy hiding under a toadstool."

Tink twitched his tail, ready to face anything I might dream up.

I went on talking to him, a habit I'd had for years, partly because he always seemed to listen. "This must be where Great-Uncle Thaddeus came to paint. These rocks are in one of his pictures, and so are those trees." I pointed to three silver birches, the biggest I'd ever seen.

Tink looked at the trees, his amber eyes wide, as if he saw things I could only imagine.

"I dreamed about this forest." I looked over my shoulder, suddenly fearful. What if Moura should come walking down the path, just as she had in my dream?

"Moura found me here," I whispered to Tink. "She wanted the witch catcher. Do you know what she did when I wouldn't give it to her? She changed into a long black snake."

I shivered and peered into the bushes, half expecting to see a snake slithering toward me. At the same moment, the woods darkened, and a cool breeze ruffled the trees, flipping the birch leaves silver side up. Thunder rumbled. From the trees, crows cawed and hurled themselves into the air, streaming away as if they knew a storm was coming.

Sure enough, well before I was halfway home, rain began pattering on the leaves. At first I thought the dense trees would shelter Tink and me, but the wind increased and the rain poured down. The steep hillside was soon awash with water. With Tink scrambling ahead, I slipped and slid my way to the top. By the time I burst out of the woods, I was soaked, and so was my cat.

Dad stood on the porch with Moura and Ciril Ashbourne. Dad saw me first. "Jen," he called, "where have you been?"

I ran up the steps and tried to dash into the house without speaking to any of them, but Dad took my arm and stopped me.

"Slow down a minute, Jen. I want you to meet our guest, Mr. Ashbourne." Turning to Moura's friend, he said, "This is my daughter, Jen."

Ciril Ashbourne's mouth twitched as if he were trying hard to smile at me. Like Moura, he was wearing tinted glasses despite the gray sky and falling rain. "It seems the storm caught you by surprise, my dear."

Moura's attempt at a smile was no better than Mr. Ashbourne's. "Have you been walking in the woods, Jen?"

When I didn't answer, she said to Dad, "The woods around here are dangerous, Hugh. Snakes, poison ivy, boggy spots. The river's treacherous, too. The current's strong, even in shallow places. Worse yet, strangers pass through now and then—tramps, I suppose. I wouldn't permit Jen to play there alone. It's simply not safe."

Dad turned from Moura to me, his face full of worry. "Maybe the woods aren't a good place to play, Jen," he said. "And from now on, please tell me where you're going when you leave the house. It worries me not to know where you are. Especially when the weather turns bad."

Dad opened the door and ushered me inside. "You'd better change your clothes. You're soaked."

Eager to escape Moura and Mr. Ashbourne, I ran upstairs with Tink. After I rubbed his fur dry, I went to the closet and grabbed my denim shirt from a hanger. The rain had cooled things off, and I was glad for a long-sleeved shirt and a pair of jeans. Leaving Tink behind, I tiptoed down to the landing and peered over the railing. Dad, Moura, and Mr. Ashbourne were now sitting in the living room drinking tea. Someone had spread Great-Uncle Thaddeus's paintings on the floor, and they seemed to be studying them.

"When you're willing to sell, I'll give you a good price for the lot," Mr. Ashbourne was saying to Dad. "As Moura surely told you, I have an interest in the realm of fairy."

Dad took another sip of tea. I wished I could see his face, but all I had was a view of the top of his head, where his hair was thinnest.

"What I really want, however, is the witch catcher your

uncle owned," Mr. Ashbourne went on. "Moura tells me it's gone missing. Has it turned up yet? I've amassed a large collection of globes, but there's always room for another. Especially if it's as fine a specimen as Moura claims it to be."

Moura smoothed her hair, held back today with silver combs, and suddenly turned to look directly at me. "Why, Jen, are you planning to join us or sit on the steps all day?"

Dad frowned, no doubt annoyed to catch me eavesdropping again. "Come and have a cup of tea, Jen," he said.

There was nothing to do but trudge down the steps and take a seat close to Dad. While Moura poured my tea, I turned to Mr. Ashbourne. "What's so special about that witch catcher?"

Mr. Ashbourne scowled at me over the rim of his cup. "I'm not accustomed to the bad manners of American children," he said to Dad. "Where I come from, children don't ask questions. They answer them."

Dad glanced at Moura, who gave him a smile and a pat on his knee. Turning to Mr. Ashbourne, she said, "Really, you're dreadfully out of touch, Ciril. This is the twenty-first century, you know. Customs change."

"Thank you for reminding me, Moura," Mr. Ashbourne said sarcastically. "But no matter what the century, manners are manners, after all."

"I assure you Jen didn't intend to be rude," Dad put in. To me he said, "Please apologize to Mr. Ashbourne."

"I was just asking him a question," I said, genuinely puzzled. "Why is that rude?"

"Never mind. It's not important." Mr. Ashbourne went back to studying me. "I shall answer your question with one of my own, young lady."

He cleared his throat, keeping his eyes on me as if he meant to read my mind. "Are you sure you don't know where the witch catcher is?"

I wanted to look away, but it was impossible. Even behind his glasses, Mr. Ashbourne's eyes held me tight, probing, probing, probing.

"If Jen knew, I'm sure she'd tell you," Dad began, but Moura hushed him with a tap on his knee with her long red fingernail.

"I won't tell you," I whispered.

"Oh, I think you will," Mr. Ashbourne said, leaning so close I could see my reflection in his glasses. Suddenly, the lenses turned iridescent. A pattern of spinning colors held me fast, made me dizzy. My arms and legs went limp.

"Indeed," Mr. Ashbourne said softly, "I believe you'll go to your room right now and fetch the witch catcher for me. You have it hidden up there, don't you, my dear?"

I shook my head, but at the same time I felt myself getting slowly to my feet. Moura began to whisper to Dad, who was too interested in what she was saying to notice me. Although I tried to resist Mr. Ashbourne, it was useless. Whether I wanted to go or not, my feet carried me upstairs.

Just as I reached the landing, I heard a loud crash. A second later, Tink came flying down the steps and disappeared.

"What the devil was that?" Mr. Ashbourne hurried past me, with Moura and Dad close behind.

I ran ahead of them to my room. The closet door was wide open, and shards of colored glass littered the floor.

"The witch catcher," I whispered. "Tink must have broken it."

Moura rushed past me and knelt to study the bits of glass. Mr. Ashbourne leaned over her, staring at the mess.

"Is it the witch catcher?" he asked Moura.

She nodded, speechless with anger.

Without noticing Moura's rage, Dad turned to me. "You lied to me, Jen. You had the witch catcher all along. And now it's broken. No one will have it."

To my surprise, Moura thrust aside my carelessly hung clothes as if she thought I might be hiding something else in the closet. She found nothing. Dropping to the floor, she looked under my bed. Nothing there, either.

Dad watched her, obviously puzzled by her behavior, but Mr. Ashbourne kept his eyes on me. "Tell me, Jen, where did you find the witch catcher?"

"In the tower," I mumbled, keeping my head down to avoid looking at those scary glasses. "Hanging in a window."

"Why did you take it?" he asked.

"It was pretty." I moved closer to Dad and pressed my face into his side, but he didn't put his arm around me or pat my head. His body was tense and unyielding. He was angry, too.

Moura grabbed my shoulder and whirled me around to

face her. Her long red nails stabbed painfully into my skin. "Do you realize what you've done?" She kept her voice low. "You've destroyed —"

Mr. Ashbourne took Moura's arm. "The child meant no harm," he said. "She thought the globe was pretty, and she wanted it. I have so many witch catchers. What's one more or less?" He smiled, but the look he gave Moura burned with anger.

Dad finally put his arm around me. "I'm sure Jen is as sorry about this as I am. But remember, Moura, I haven't decided what to sell and what to keep. So the broken globe is Jen's loss. No one else's."

"Of course, Hugh." Moura managed to smile at him. "Forgive me. As a dealer in antiques, I simply can't bear to see valuable objects used as playthings by careless children."

"I wasn't playing with it," I said, stung by her implications, "and I'm not a careless child. I put the witch catcher in a safe place. It's not my fault Tink broke it."

"Perhaps we should return to the living room and finish our tea," Mr. Ashbourne suggested. "I'm still hoping you'll decide to part with those wonderful paintings, Hugh."

Mr. Ashbourne led the way downstairs. Before we reached the bottom, Moura took my arm and whispered, "If you see anything strange, tell me at once. You could be in great danger, you foolish girl."

I stopped on the landing and stared at her. "What do you mean?"

“I told you the purpose of witch catchers,” she said. “When one is broken, odd things happen.”

“The witch escapes?” Goose bumps sprang up on my arms, but I forced myself to laugh. “Surely you don’t believe in evil spirits.”

Moura looked at me, clearly not amused. “You’re ignorant as well as foolish and dishonest.”

With that, she swept down the steps to join Dad and Mr. Ashbourne. Her hair and skirt floated out behind her as if she were sinking into the shadows at the foot of the stairs.

“The tea’s cold, Jen,” Dad said. “Would you mind making a fresh pot?”

Glad to be excused, I left the three of them in the living room. After I filled the kettle and set it on the stove, I collapsed on a chair. My head ached, and my legs felt weak, as if I were coming down with the flu.

What had just happened? I’d been without any will of my own—Mr. Ashbourne must have hypnotized me somehow. I’d been completely under his power, as mindless as a zombie. Those glasses—had I imagined the way they’d changed color?

The worst part was Dad—he hadn’t noticed a thing out of the ordinary. Had he been bewitched, too?

I hugged myself and shivered uncontrollably, more frightened than cold.

“Jen,” Dad called from the living room, “the kettle’s boiling.”

His voice and the loud whistle from the kettle roused me. Still shaky, I got to my feet and filled the teapot with boiling water.

Tink emerged from his hiding place and rubbed against my legs.

"I suppose you're apologizing," I said. "But it'll take a lot more than that to make up for what you've done."

Tink purred loudly and wound himself around me as if he were trying extra special hard to convince me he was truly sorry. But he didn't fool me. No cat was ever sorry for anything it did.

I stooped down and looked Tink in the eye. "Why did you jump up on that shelf? You broke the witch catcher, the most beautiful thing I've ever owned. Worse yet, now everyone knows I lied about having it. And do you know what's even more terrible?"

Tink mewed and bumped his face against mine, waiting to be told.

"Moura says something scary might happen because it's broken." I rubbed Tink under his chin, and he purred louder. "Of course, she's lying, but still— If I were you, I'd watch out, Tink. You're the one who broke it, you know. Not me."

Tink went on purring as if to say he couldn't care less about broken witch catchers.

Straightening up, I stared out the window. The glass was streaked with water, and the rain fell hard enough to blur the tower and the trees and the sky. A few crows stalked across the lawn, heads down, sodden black feathers dripping. Thunder clapped, and raggedy lines of lightning zigzagged across the sky. In the living room, Dad laughed at something Moura said, and Mr. Ashbourne joined in.

I looked down at Tink. "They don't need me, do they? I bet Dad doesn't even miss me."

Tink purred again, and I picked him up, grateful for his warm weight and soft fur. He relaxed in my arms, and I rocked him as if he were still a little kitten. "You're such a bad cat," I whispered. "Such a bad, bad cat—but I love you anyway."

He snuggled in my arms, pressing his warm body against my chest, and purred even louder.

"Jen," Dad called again. "Isn't that tea ready yet?"

I put Tink down and picked up the teapot. Feeling like Cinderella, I carried the tray carefully toward the living room and Dad's guests.

8

THE RAIN STOPPED about the time Moura and Mr. Ashbourne got up to leave. We walked outside to say goodbye—me gladly, Dad sadly, despite Moura's quick kiss.

After the sleek little car disappeared around a curve, Dad turned to me. "It's not like you to lie or be secretive, Jen. We—"

"'We'?" I scowled at him. "'*We*' is you and Moura now, not you and me."

"Jen—"

But I was already gone, heading toward the woods with Tink at my heels.

"Come back here!" Dad called. "You heard what Moura said."

Ignoring my father, I plunged into the wet, gloomy forest. After the rain, the air smelled damper than ever. The leaves dripped, and when I got to the stream, it ran high and fast, foaming around the rocks. I sat on one of the boulders and watched Tink try to explore the underbrush without getting wet.

If Moura thought she could scare me into staying home

like a good little girl, she didn't know me. Besides, I wanted to get away from Dad. He wasn't himself anymore. Moura and her witchy ways had changed him and everything else—including me. I'd never lied to my father before, never kept things from him. But that witch catcher—I'd disobeyed him to get it. And then I couldn't give it up. Not with Moura around. She would've persuaded Dad to give it to her.

Suddenly, Tink ran out of the bushes. A small, thin girl dressed in rags and tatters of filthy clothing followed him. The dense shade gave her pale skin a greenish tint. Or maybe she was just dirty. Her mouth was wide, her lips thin, her eyes oddly slanted, and her hair was a tangled mass of black curls. She was the weirdest kid I'd ever seen. Yet she was oddly familiar, like something I'd seen in a dream.

To my surprise, Tink went up to her and rubbed against her legs and purred so loudly I felt a stab of jealousy. I'd never seen him be that friendly to anyone but me.

"Hello there, boyo." The girl leaned down and rubbed her face against the cat's face. "Good kitty," she crooned.

"Tink," I called, sliding down off the boulder. "Come here."

Tink glanced at me, but he stayed where he was, contrary as ever.

The girl straightened up and turned to me. "Where's the old man gone?" Her voice was low and hoarse, raspy but not harsh.

"The old man?" I echoed, a little scared of her odd appearance but too curious to run back to the house and Dad.

"Him who lives up yonder in the castle. Him who built the tower."

"Great-Uncle Thaddeus? Mr. Mostyn? Is that who you mean?"

"Mostyn, yes. Him. Where is he?"

"He died a couple of years ago," I told her. "He left his house to my father, so we're living there now."

"Mostyn died?" Her face turned pale under the dirt. "Are ye sure?"

"He was very old, you know. Ancient. Almost a hundred."

"A hundred years. . . . Fancy thinking that's old." She sighed and shook her head. "Well, he were a right dafty fellow, but at least he kept me safe. Now I reckon it's up to ye."

"You want *me* to keep you safe?" I stared at her. "Safe from what?"

"From the lady, of course." The girl looked around uneasily as if she expected to see someone lurking in the woods. "*Her* who's been here three times now, swishing around, seeking and prying and sniffing for me."

A little shiver raced up and down my spine. "Are you talking about Moura Winters?"

"Hush," the girl said. "That be *her*, but be careful how ye speak. Names have power, ye know."

She peered into the woods again, her body tense, poised to run. "They be a bad pair, *her* and the collector. *Him* with the magic spectacles. They be witches, brimful of evil and wickedness."

I drew in my breath. Hadn't I known from the moment I saw Moura that she was dangerous? And Mr. Ashbourne—those scary glasses, the way he'd made me lead him upstairs just as if he'd cast a spell on me.

But how could they be witches? Confused, I looked around at the familiar world. A gray sky like thousands I'd seen before hid the sun. Trees swayed in the breeze as they always did. Rainwater dripped from the leaves with a familiar *pit-a-pat.* Two squirrels chased each other around a tree trunk. Deeper in the woods, a bird called. Everything was just as it should be, just as it had always been. Ordinary. Safe.

Yet just a few feet away stood an odd, raggedy girl. Nothing about *her* was ordinary. Not the tattered clothes she wore, not the things she said, not the odd words she used. With a shock, I realized she looked like the girl in Uncle Thaddeus's painting—half wild, not quite human.

I took a step backward, suddenly uneasy. Maybe a little afraid. Except for Tink, I was alone, deep in the woods, far from the house. No one knew where I was, not even Dad.

I was tempted to grab Tink and run, but something about the girl held me there. She didn't seem dangerous, just strange. Mysterious. Puzzling.

"Who are you?" I whispered. "Where did you come from? How do you know Great-Uncle Thaddeus and Moura? Why—"

"Them that asks too many questions must wait for answers." With the grace of a cat, the girl reached for a low branch and swung herself up into an oak tree. Perched above my head, thin legs dangling, she peered down at me.

"Yer first question be the easiest one," she said. "I'm called Kieryn. And ye be Jen."

"How do you know my name?"

A sly little grin tweaked the corners of her wide mouth. "I been in yer bedroom, ye great ninny, listening to ye babble away to yer cat. He knowed I were there, crying and begging to be let out, but ye mistook me for a bug. A dimbob cicada. An uglier creature I never seen—red eyes it's got."

When Kieryn paused to take a breath, I asked, "What are you talking about?"

"Ye great booby, ain't ye figured it out yet?" Kieryn laughed down at me, revealing a mouthful of small white teeth. "I were in that skitzy witch trap ye took from the tower and hung in yer window, the one Tink busted. Smarter than ye he is."

Tink climbed up the tree and stretched out on the limb beside Kieryn. I reached for him. "Come here."

He glanced at me and twitched his tail, but he stayed where he was.

Kieryn looked down at me. "Ye don't believe me, do ye?"

I shook my head. "You're almost as big as I am. How could you possibly have been inside that little globe?"

Kieryn's small, dirty feet swung back and forth. Every now and then she glanced around, as if she expected to see someone sneaking toward us through the trees. "Mostyn showed me them pretty colors all spinning and shining, and in I went through the spout—*poof!* from the size I be now to something no bigger than a nandy caterpillar."

"I don't believe you." That's what I said, but it wasn't entirely true. More and more I *wanted* to believe her. After all, we had an enemy in common. "For one thing," I went on, "if you'd really been trapped in that globe, you'd be a witch—or an evil spirit."

Kieryn threw back her head and laughed. "Is that what *her* told ye?"

"Yes, but—"

She leaned out of the tree and regarded me with a fierce scowl. "Truly true, I were in the globe, but *her* lied to ye about the traps and what they catch. I ain't a witch, nor be I evil. Those snarky traps suck in everything that's magic—good as well as bad." She flipped around and hung by her knees, her face level with mine. "Remember this, Jen. Witches *always* lie. It's against their very blood and bone to tell the truth."

Confused, I backed away from that odd little upside-down face.

"Surely yer not afeared of me, Jen?" She grinned her sly little grin and swung back and forth by her knees. "I mean ye no harm, ye great ninny. I swear it."

"Of course I'm not scared of you," I said, hoping she couldn't hear my heart going *boom-diddyboom*, like a big bass drum. "Why should I be?"

"What if *I* be a witch?" Kieryn dropped from the tree like a ripe apple and landed on the ground beside me. This close she smelled like cinnamon and dust.

"But you just told me you're not a witch."

Kieryn laughed and clapped her hands. "Yes, but I also told ye witches lie."

Suddenly serious, she studied my face so long I had to look away in embarrassment. Finally, she turned to Tink, still stretched out on the low branch. "Can I trust her?"

The cat tipped his head ever so slightly in my direction, and purred.

Kieryn nodded, satisfied. "First, ye must swear on yer very heart and soul never, ever, *ever* to tell anyone about me—or who I be. Not *her*. Not *him*. Not even yer own dear daddy."

Almost hypnotized by the intensity of Kieryn's gaze, I took a deep breath and whispered, "I swear on my very heart and soul never to tell anyone about you. Never, ever, *ever*."

Kieryn hesitated, as if she still didn't quite trust me. Tink purred and dropped down from the tree into my arms. "Well," Kieryn said to the cat, "if ye trust her, I reckon I will, too, for cats be good at judging who's good and who's bad."

Glancing over her shoulder, she studied the woods behind her as if to make sure no one hid behind the trees. "First ye must know my kinkind go by many names in yer world. 'Travelers,' some call us, because we come from far away.

Others call us 'the people' or 'the strangers' because they're scared to say our real name. A few call us 'friends.' But, Jen, listen close and I'll tell ye the truth."

She pressed her mouth against my ear and whispered, "What I be is fairy."

I drew away from the warm breath tingling in my ear. Almost as if she stood beside me, I heard Moura's voice saying, *Fairies aren't the dear little creatures you imagine them to be. . . . they are malicious, spiteful, and completely untrustworthy.*

"You can't be a fairy," I whispered, frightened now of her strangeness, her pointed face, her odd eyes. Perhaps Moura had been trying to protect me, not harm me.

Misunderstanding what I'd said, Kieryn shook her head in disgust. "If ye think my kinkind be no bigger than dimbob butterflies flitting about rose gardens, ye been reading the wrong books. We be full-size folk—clever as foxes, good at tricks and magic, flummoxers and rascals from way back."

I stared at her, still fearful, unsure. Moura's words ran round and round in my head—*wicked, beyond imagining. . . . She's a fairy I wouldn't want to meet in a dark wood.*

"'Tis *her*, ain't it?" Kieryn's small face screwed itself into a fierce grimace. "Ye been listening to the lies *her* tells about my kinkind. *Her*, our enemy, our foe. *Her*, a witch of the twelfth degree. Listen to yer ownself, Jen—what do ye think of me?"

She's scared, I heard my own voice in my head, *not wicked.*

That's what I'd told Dad about the girl in the painting. It's what I thought, not what Moura wanted me to think.

Still a little uneasy, I managed a small smile. "I believe you're a fairy," I said, "but you're not evil, and I'm not afraid of you."

"There now, that be better," Kieryn said cheerfully. "Never let a witch into yer head, Jen—especially one as twelve times wicked as *her* be."

Somewhere behind me in the still woods, I heard Dad call my name. "It's my father," I told Kieryn. "He's looking for me."

Without a word, Kieryn picked up Tink and peered at me, her pointed face framed by his ears. Silently she ran her hands over him, his back, his tummy, his head, legs, and tail. While she stroked him, she began humming to herself. The woods grew still and the air felt thick, the way it does before a thunderstorm. My scalp tingled, and the hair on my arms rose.

Suddenly, Kieryn's body wavered as if I were looking at her through a campfire on a hot summer day. With a jolt strong enough for me to feel, she disappeared. In her place was a scrawny gray kitten with green eyes.

Face to face with the kitten, Tink purred and touched his nose to hers. Not me. I got to my feet and backed away in disbelief.

"Don't be afeared," the kitten cried in a raspy voice. "I'm still me."

"How?" I stammered. "How did you do that?"

The kitten shrugged. "I reckon if I understood the whys and wherefores of magic, I couldn't do it no more."

Dad called again, closer.

"Take me home with ye," Kieryn whispered. "Keep me safe from *her* and *him*."

I picked her up. Her body was as warm and fuzzy and soft as a real kitten's. "What shall I tell Dad?"

"Tell him ye found me in the woods," Kieryn said. "Ask him to let ye keep me. But don't call me Kieryn. *Her* knows me by that name."

"How about Misty? It suits your gray fur."

Kieryn wrinkled her pink nose. "Truth's bells, is that the best ye can do?"

I thought a second. "Mist, then. Is that better?"

"I suppose it'll do for a wee while."

"Jen!" Dad called. "Jen, where are you?" He sounded both worried and cross.

"Coming, Dad," I called. "Coming!"

I ran to meet my father. Kieryn clung to my shirt, her kitten claws digging into my skin like tiny pricking pins. Tink bounded along ahead, tail waving proudly.

I met Dad at a curve in the path. "Where have you been, Jen? I told you not to go running off."

"I'm sorry," I apologized. "I won't do it again. I promise."

"What's that you've got?" Dad peered at the kitten cuddled in my arms.

I held her up so he could see how pretty she was. "This is Mist. I found her in the woods down by the stream. She's half starved, poor little thing."

Dad shook his head. "And you want to keep her, I suppose?"

"Please, Dad, please? She's so sweet."

"What about Tink?"

"He loves her." I knelt down and Tink rubbed his nose against Kieryn's tiny pink nose. "See?"

Dad reached out and stroked Kieryn's little head. Immediately, she began to purr as loudly as she could.

"Listen to that. She loves you, Dad."

Dad laughed. "Cats are such phonies. Once I say yes, she'll probably never come near me again."

Kieryn kept purring, louder and louder till her whole skinny body vibrated.

"Okay, okay," Dad said. "But we'll have to take her to the vet first thing tomorrow to make sure she's healthy. She'll need shots, too. And then, when she's older, we'll have her spayed."

Kieryn immediately turned off her purr machine and pulled away from Dad's hand. I was sure she was struggling not to hiss at him.

He laughed again. "You'd almost think she understands English."

I smiled down at Kieryn. "Cats understand more than people realize."

"Let's go back to the house," Dad said, "and feed that poor starved creature."

The path through the woods was too narrow to walk side by side, so I followed Dad home, plodding slowly uphill. On either side, oaks, maples, and birches towered over us, blocking the sky with their leafy branches. Thick moss covered the earth and grew soft on the trees. Boulders reared from the ground, dappled green and blue and yellow with moss and lichen. Ferns grew tall and lush. It was an enchanted forest, just as I'd thought when I'd first seen it. Anything could happen here.

In fact, it already had.

9

WHILE TINK WATCHED, Dad filled a bowl with dry cat food for Kieryn. When he set it in front of her, she sniffed it suspiciously and recoiled.

"What's the matter, my lady?" Dad asked. "Isn't Tink's food good enough for you?"

Kieryn mewed pitifully and gave me an angry look. "Maybe she's not used to dry food," I suggested. "What about milk?"

Dad selected a small bowl from the cupboard. He hesitated in front of the refrigerator. "It seems to me I read somewhere milk isn't good for cats."

"But she's so little. Surely it can't hurt her."

Dad sighed and poured some milk into the bowl. When he set it in front of Kieryn, she drank it greedily.

"I hope it doesn't make her sick," he said.

"Oh, Dad, you're such a worrywart." I hugged him.

He shrugged and smiled. "Just because I'm a worrywart doesn't mean there's nothing to worry about."

I watched him make a pot of tea for the two of us. The rain had begun again. A strong wind drove sheets of water against the windows and lashed the trees and bushes. Lightning whipped across the sky, and thunder boomed.

Dad looked out the back door. "I love a good storm," he said.

"What would happen if lightning struck the tower?" I asked him.

"See those metal poles on the roof?" He pointed. "Those are lightning rods. They're designed to redirect the lightning away from a building and into the ground." He smiled. "Great-Uncle Thaddeus thought of everything."

I nodded and sipped my tea, sweet with honey and milk. It was cozy to be at the kitchen table with Dad. Kieryn sat in my lap, purring, and Tink crouched on the windowsill, peering out at the wet world. If only Moura hadn't come into our lives, everything would be perfect.

As if he'd heard me think Moura's name, Dad said, "I hope the weather doesn't keep Moura from joining us for dinner tonight."

I felt Kieryn's body tense. "She was here just last night," I said. "And this morning. Why is she coming again tonight?"

Dad hesitated and stirred more honey into his tea. "Well, we agreed it would make sense for her to live here while she inventories the contents of the house." He went on stirring his tea, his eyes on the cup, not on me. "After Moura appraises their value, I can make an educated decision about what I want to sell and what I want to keep."

"But she has a house! And a shop, too. Why should she stay with us?"

Kieryn put her paws on the table and looked at Dad as if she were as upset as I was.

Still avoiding my eyes, Dad stirred more honey into his tea. "We're so far from town, it makes perfect sense for Moura to live here, instead of driving back and forth between our place and hers."

"Where is she sleeping?"

"She'll have her own room," Dad said quickly. "It will be perfectly proper, Jen."

"What if I say I don't want her here?" My voice rose.

"Moura's my fiancée, Jen." Dad set his cup down and looked me straight in the eye. His voice was patient but firm. "You'll have to get used to sharing me with her."

"But—"

He raised his hand to silence me. "Believe me, Moura understands. She'll do everything she can to make things easy for you."

Holding Kieryn tight, I jumped to my feet. "Well, I won't make things easy for her!"

Without waiting for him to reply, I ran to my room, with Tink at my heels. Slamming the door shut, I sank down on my bed and wept. Kieryn touched my shoulder.

"I'm sorry for ye and yer dad," she whispered. "*Her* has wicked strong magic."

I nodded. No one had to tell *me* about Moura's power. It

was Dad who needed to be told. But he wouldn't listen to a word against her.

I raised my head and looked at Kieryn. She was in her own shape again, crouched on the bed and shivering in her rags and tatters.

"You can't go around dressed like that." I pulled some clothes out of my drawer—a T-shirt, underwear, shorts. "Here, put these on."

Turning her back, Kieryn peeled off her clothing, yanked on mine, then looked at herself in the mirror. "Great purple toads!" she exclaimed. "I be as ugly as a wergle in these here boshy clothes."

She was right. Even in their wretched condition, her own clothes had looked better on her than mine did. Shorts and a T-shirt merely accentuated her strangeness. It would be hard to convince anyone she was an ordinary human being. Not with those eyes and that skin.

I yanked open the bottom drawer and pulled out a long old-fashioned nightgown. The bodice was pleated in tiny folds, and its neck, cuffs, and hem were ruffled and trimmed with lace. I'd picked it from a catalog and Dad had given it to me for Christmas. I'd been saving it for a special occasion. This was definitely as special as occasions come.

I held it up for Kieryn to see. "Is this better?"

Her wide mouth spread into a big smile of pure delight. "Oh, aye, Jen, aye. It's purely proper, and pretty as well."

She shed the shorts and T-shirt and slipped the gown over her head. Twirling around, she admired her reflection in the mirror. “Thank’ee, thank’ee,” she said. “I feels more like my true self now.”

As she spun, I glimpsed a silver chain around her neck. “What’s that?” I asked.

Kieryn’s hand flew to her chest as if to hide the necklace. “What’s what?”

“The chain around your neck.”

“I didn’t mean for ye to see it,” Kieryn said in a low voice. “But maybe it’s best ye know.”

Reaching inside the nightgown, she slowly pulled out the delicate silver chain. On it hung a stone the color of the midnight sky, set in twisted strands of silver as delicate as cobwebs. It was similar to Moura’s red pendant, but made with greater skill. A shape like a tiny star glimmered in the stone’s depth.

“Mam gave me this afore she sent me here. Without it, I can’t go home. The door is sealed against all—even me.” Kieryn held the stone to the light and stared into it as if she saw her world there.

I moved a little closer. “I don’t understand. Why did your mother send you here?”

“It be a long story and hard to tell, but it was during the Third War of the Witches that our troubles began,” Kieryn said. “My father, the king, was newly dead, and the witches rose up, stronger than ever. They come after Brynn and me, planning to kill us, I expect, on account of our royal blood. Mam led us deep, deep into the forest to a tall oak tree. Its trunk was so big, ten folk couldn’t have joined hands and reached around it. Ye might say it were the king of the trees. Mam held up the pendant, and a door opened in the tree, a door into the darkest dark ye ever saw.

Kieryn shuddered, and Tink crept into her lap, purring as if to comfort her. "Mam slipped the chain over my head. 'Guard this stone well,' she said, 'for ye can't come home without it.' With that, she pushed us through the door and shouted 'Run, run, and keep running till ye come out the other side.' And we did—my brother, Brynn, and me and our three aunties. We ran through the dark and the cold, thinking Mam were following us."

She paused to wipe her eyes on the sleeve of the nightgown. "We five come out into a forest, but Mam weren't with us. I started to run back into the dark for her, but the tree closed itself up all ordinary-like, and there was only bark where the door had been. Brynn and I beat on it with our fists and called Mam, but she didn't open the door, she didn't come out."

Kieryn turned her head away, but even with her back to me, I knew she was crying and didn't want me to see. "I tried the stone, but it didn't work. The aunties said it were too soon to go home."

I put my arm around her skinny little shoulders, and Tink nestled closer, purring and rubbing his face against hers. He always sensed when I needed comforting and did his best to make me feel better. Now he was doing the same for Kieryn.

"Oh, Jen," she whispered, "we was in a strange place, not

our world, but yers. All dark and sad, with no magic—and no Mam."

Taking Tink with her, Kieryn slid off the bed and went to the window. "Then we saw that tower." She pointed across the yard. "It had the bosky feel of magic—but good or bad, we couldn't tell. An old man with a beard were standing in the doorway, staring at us like he could scarce believe his eyes. It were Mostyn . . . yer dimbob uncle. He called out to us, all nicey-nice, but we didn't dare trust him. Off we ran, down the hill, and into the woods."

Kieryn clenched her fists. "That's when we spied *her* and *him* and the hound snarking through the trees. Somehow they'd come through the door, searching, seeking, sniffing, as witches do. Lucky for us, our three aunties know plenty of magic, more than Brynn and me, 'cause we're just young. They made hiding spells to keep us all safe."

Kieryn came back to the bed. "After that we was cautious," she went on. "We kept a close watch on the tower and this big old house. We knew yer uncle had a gift, else he wouldn't have seen us so quick. Most of yer kind are such dimbobs they never notice us passing through yer world. Too smart he were. Too learned in our ways."

I remembered the old books in the tower, filled with strange letters like the runes carved on the door. Uncle Thaddeus had stayed up there night and day, Dad said. He was eccentric, odd, mistrusted by the people in town. Had he been studying magic? Witchcraft?

"I suspect there be a bit of yer uncle in ye," Kieryn said. "Somehow ye knew to hide that globe from *her,* ye knew not to trust *her* or *him.* But ye trust me, do ye not?"

I forced myself to return Kieryn's steady gaze. "Yes," I said. "I do trust you." But even as I spoke, I felt as if I was wading into a dark pool; with every step I took, I sank deeper into the murky water.

"But smart as that old rascal was, he weren't no match for *her,*" Kieryn went on with her story. "Soon *her* came calling on him, all pretty pretty and sweet. In a blink of a lizard's eye, she wove her fossicky spells, till yer uncle couldn't tell a snog from a wergle. She warned him that strange creatures had been seen near his tower. They was evil, she said. Dangerous. They came from another world, they wasn't human like him and *her. Her* gave the little-wit dozens of them pisky traps, all hidden away in velvet bags so she couldn't see them and get caught herself. Hang the traps in the woods, she said. And that's just what Mostyn done."

Kieryn rose from the bed and prowled around my room, as restless as Tink. "Oh, so pretty them traps were, like they had rainbows inside, swinging from branches, tinkling like bells when they bumped up against each other, asparkle with sunshine by day and moonshine by night. Nary a one of us, not even the aunties, could stay away from them skitzy things. They pulled us and tugged at us. First Brynn got sucked in, then the aunties. I were last, holding fast to a tree. But even with my eyes tight shut, I could see them colors in my mind, drawing me closer, closer."

She wrapped her arms around herself and shuddered. "Just as I lost my grip on the tree, I opened my eyes and there was Mostyn, staring at me like I were a dream come true. Then—*poof!*—I were inside the globe, looking out at him. He stuck his boshy old face up close to the glass and told me he'd give the others to *her* but aimed to keep me for hisself."

Kieryn scowled. "It weren't on account he were a good man and he were aiming to save me," she said. "No, that weren't it at all. Mostyn wanted me because I were a right interesting specimen, and he wanted to study me."

She sighed and stopped pacing long enough to look out the window. "The next day, *her* came calling, and Mostyn gave her four full traps and the empty ones as well, all packed up in them velvet bags. He told her that were all he had. A good lie for me that was, but bad for Brynn and the aunties. Away they went with *her*, a clinking and a clanking in the bags till I don't wonder they was all sick."

Kieryn fell silent for a moment. Tink rubbed against her ankles, purring, and she picked him up.

"*Her* didn't believe Mostyn," she said. "Back *her* came time and time again, always asking for me, and Mostyn always saying he caught but four demons and already gave them to her. Soon *her* was living in the house, just like she is now."

"Did my uncle love her, too? Just like Dad?"

"I reckon he thought he did, for surely he were under her spell, just like yer daddy. After all, ain't love potions witches' work?"

"But if she enchanted my uncle, why didn't he give her the trap?"

"He'd learned himself some magic from them big old bosky books in the tower, just enough, I reckon, to keep *her* from getting me. Meanwhile, he'd started painting those pictures of me—pictures he kept hidden from *her.* But *her* kept on with the nicey-nice, sugartime sweet, hoping to break his spell. Then one day *her* got tired of waiting and done a nasty that made Mostyn go all sideways and crooked like. He couldn't walk or talk right afterward, but afore she'd done her bad spell on him, he'd sealed the tower door agin her with a charm he knew, and she couldn't get in to fossick me away."

Kieryn perched on the edge of the bed and gazed at me. "So there I stayed, watching day to night, day to night through them swirly colors, with my head getting more and more wooly. Till ye came and stole me away to yer room and hung me all secret in the window and never knowed I was inside watching ye and crying to be let out."

Kieryn smiled. "Ye and Tink done me a good deed, and I won't forget it, but I got something more to ask of ye. A favor, like. Friend to friend." She twirled a lock of hair around her finger and pulled it tight. "It be a hard favor, Jen, but I need yer help to rescue my brother and my aunties."

Caught up in her story, I squeezed Kieryn's hands. She was my friend, she'd just said so, a friend like no other I'd ever have. Without thinking, I said, "Of course I will."

She hesitated a moment and then said, "I'll be leading ye

into peril, Jen. *Her* be more dangerous than ye know. We must be ever on guard against *her* and *him* and their fossicky ways. They want me terrible bad."

I shivered and held Kieryn's hands tighter. Moura was my enemy as well as hers. No matter how dangerous the witch was, I had to save Dad—and Kieryn, too. For once in my life, I needed to be brave. Truly brave.

Suddenly, Kieryn tensed. "*Her*'s coming," she whispered. "I hear *her* car. Quick, take the pendant. Hide it. Keep it safe. It be the key to my world."

She thrust the stone at me, and I closed my hand around it cautiously, almost fearfully. It felt warm and smooth—and magical.

"*Her* needs this to get her wickedly bad self back to our world," Kieryn whispered. "Ye must not let *her* get it. *Her* means naught but harm to my kinkind."

I looked around my room, seeking a hiding place. My mother's old jewelry box sat on my bureau, filled with strings of beads, tarnished chains, and an assortment of bracelets and earrings.

"That's the first place *her* will look," Kieryn said.

I shook my head. "I read a story once about a stolen letter. Everybody was hunting for it, but they never thought to look in the most obvious place—the letter rack."

I made a little hole in the lining of the box, pushed the pendant inside, and dumped the jewelry back inside. "There!"

Kieryn looked skeptical. "*Her* and *him* are good sniffers, ye know. And so's the hound." Dropping to the floor, she crawled under my bed and pried up a piece of floorboard. She then held out her hand for the box.

Kieryn lowered it into the space she'd made and laid the board over it. She remained under the bed for a few moments more, chanting words I couldn't understand.

"There." She crawled out with a grin on her face. "I put my best spell on it. Let's hope *her* won't find it."

We went back to the window. Moura's sleek little car drew up to the house, its headlights dim in the rain. Wordlessly, Kieryn, Tink, and I watched the car's door open. The interior light came on, revealing Moura in her usual glamorous red and black—a long, sweeping black skirt, a white lacy blouse, and a black jacket patterned with red flames.

"Witch colors," Kieryn hissed.

Cadoc leapt out of the car and watched Dad run through the rain to help Moura with her suitcases.

"She's not wearing her tinted glasses," I said.

"They keep *her* from seeing the colors in the witch trap," Kieryn whispered. "*Her* don't need 'em now the trap's been broke."

Hoping Dad wouldn't call me to join him and Moura, I grabbed a book and flung myself on the bed. Kieryn curled up beside me, and in an instant transformed herself. Now she looked for all the world like an ordinary little gray cat.

"Tell me about yer mam," she said. "She must not be hereabouts or yer daddy wouldn't be all sheep-eyed, lovey-dovey over *her*."

I sighed. "My mother died when I was a baby."

Kieryn snuggled closer. "Oh, poor Jen. If I knew I'd never see Mam again, my heart would break into a million billion pieces." Her voice was as comforting as a cat's purr.

I swallowed hard. "I never even knew her." I picked up the picture on the chest beside my bed. "This is how my mother looked just after she married Dad. They were in Bermuda, on their honeymoon."

Kieryn studied the photo. My mother wore tan shorts and a red T-shirt. She was laughing, her head tilted, long blond hair swinging out to the side. Behind her was the ocean and a blue sky.

"She were beautiful, Jen."

"She was." I put Mom's picture on the chest and studied her as I had so often. I longed to know what lay behind that laughing face—her thoughts, her feelings, what she loved, what she didn't love. But she was gone from this world. She couldn't answer my questions; she couldn't help me. And she couldn't help Dad.

Catlike, Kieryn rubbed her furry gray face against mine. "We'll save yer father, Jen, I promise ye. *Her* won't have him. We'll put an end to *her* and her skitzy ways. I got some magic, ye know."

I lay on my bed, with Tink purring on one side and Kieryn purring on the other. For the moment, I felt warm and safe. Kieryn would help me. Somehow we'd defeat Moura.

Kieryn nudged my book with her paw. "Read to me," she whispered. "I ain't heard a story for longer than long."

"It's *The Woman in White,*" I told her. "I borrowed it from

Uncle Thaddeus's library. I haven't read much, so I'll go back and start at the beginning."

We hadn't gotten to the end of the first chapter when Dad called me. "Jen, please come down and set the table. Dinner's almost ready."

I didn't answer, just went on reading. Dad called again, closer this time. It sounded as if he was at the foot of the steps.

Kieryn put her paw on the book. "It's best ye go," she whispered. "Next thing he'll be up here, fussy fussing at ye. *Her* will be on his side, ye know, always trying to make him love *her* best."

"Dad would never let Moura come between us," I protested. "I'm his daughter. He loves me."

"Don't make him be choosing between *her* and ye. *Her* has spells and magic and charms. Ye got nothing but yer little girly self."

I scowled at the gray cat. "Dad would choose me, I know he would." But even as I spoke, my voice faltered. I'd read fairy tales where the evil stepmother convinced the father to abandon his children. With Kieryn in cat form sitting beside me, fairy tales were easier to believe than true stories.

I closed the book with an angry snap and stood up, unwilling to listen to another word. Kieryn had frightened me. Suppose Moura cast a spell so strong that Dad stopped loving me?

At the door, I looked back at Kieryn. "Are you coming downstairs with me?"

"Nay." She curled into a soft ball of gray fur and shut her eyes. "*Her* hates cats. And so do her hound."

"Jen, do I have to come up there?" Dad shouted.

Slowly I went out into the hall and looked down the stairs at Dad. Moura stood beside him, her arm linked with his, her face unreadable. Without her glasses, I got the full benefit of her piercing stare. Cadoc stood beside his mistress, his narrow nose pointed up at me, his eyes as sharp as hers.

Knowing what I knew now, I didn't dare return Moura's stare. For all I knew, she could read my innermost thoughts. Turning to Dad, I said, "Sorry, I wanted to finish the chapter I was reading."

Moura flashed her humorless smile at me. "Oh, I loved to read when I was your age. In fact, I still do. A good book, a cozy room, a cat or two curled next to you—what could be more delightful on a rainy night?"

The sound of her voice scratched my nerves like a cat's claws, but Dad gave Moura a tender look before grinning at me. "You see, Jen? She'll fit right into our household. Think how pleasant our evenings will be, the three of us reading by the fire, cats on our laps, a dog at our feet."

I longed to tell Dad I preferred the evenings of the past when he and I read together, just the two of us, but I restrained myself. Smiling so stiffly that my face hurt, I joined the two of them.

10

WHILE DAD GRILLED steaks on the terrace behind the house, I set the table with Great-Uncle Thaddeus's beautiful old silver and china. I could hear Moura's voice but not what she was saying. Dad said something, and the two of them laughed. The sound made me feel lonely, shut out, unwanted. I looked up at Great-Uncle Thaddeus's portrait. "This is all your fault. Why did you believe that woman?"

When the portrait failed to respond, I realized I'd fully expected it to. Anything could happen in this house. Portraits might speak, ghosts rattle chains in the dark hallways, blue lights flit from room to room, footsteps echo, doors open and shut.

I walked closer to the portrait and glared at the old man. "Well?" I asked. "Don't you have anything to say for yourself?"

"Jen?"

I whirled around to see Moura in the doorway, arms crossed, staring at me. "I thought I heard you talking to someone," she said.

"No." I shook my head and tried to laugh. "I was just muttering to myself."

"About what?" She stepped closer. I could smell the musky scent of her perfume.

"It was Tink." The cat had appeared from nowhere, winding around my ankles and mewing. "He was about to jump up on the table. He's not supposed to do that. So I was telling him what a bad cat he is."

Moura glanced at the cat. "You are indeed a bad cat, Tink."

Tink lashed his tail, but he stood his ground. Moura turned away from him, uninterested. "Speaking of cats, your father tells me you found a kitten today." She smiled her shivery smile.

"A little gray one," I said. "I named her Mist."

"I've heard there's a colony of feral cats in the woods," Moura said softly. "You can't tame a wild cat, you know. They don't trust people. I'm surprised it came near you."

"Mist's very sweet. She's not a bit wild."

"She may be carrying disease. Fleas, too." Moura touched my cheek lightly with a long red fingernail. "Why, that kitten could turn on you and rake your face open with her claws."

My skin tingled where she'd touched it, and I drew back from her.

Dad stepped into the room just in time to hear Moura's last words. "I don't think the cat's vicious," he said. "Anyway, we're taking her to the vet first thing tomorrow."

"That's a very good idea." Moura flashed her chilly smile at Dad. "Perhaps I could take a look at her after dinner. I know something about cats."

Cadoc entered the room then, moving as silently as a

shadow, and lay down beside Moura. Tink flowed out the other door and vanished into the kitchen. Moura would not look at the kitten, I decided, no matter what Dad said.

I ate silently so I could listen to Moura and Dad. Mostly they discussed books and poetry, a play they'd both seen at the Kennedy Center years ago, movies they'd enjoyed. Nobody noticed I had nothing to say. Nobody looked at me. Nobody asked me a question or sought my opinion. I might as well have stayed upstairs reading to Kieryn.

When we'd finished dinner, Dad turned to me. At last, I thought, he's going to include me in the conversation. I sat up straight and smiled at him, waiting for a question.

"How about clearing the table, Jen, and bringing in dessert?" he asked.

I stared at him, too hurt to say a word. Next, I supposed he'd tell me to eat my meals in the kitchen. A good servant knows her place. Instead of jumping up, I toyed with a bit of broccoli, pushing it this way and that with my fork.

"Jen." Dad leaned toward me. "Will you please do as you're told?"

Under the table, near my feet, I felt Cadoc stir. I pushed my chair back and stood up. "I'm not hungry," I said as calmly as I could. "I'm going to bed."

Without looking at either of them, I left the dining room. Let them get their own dessert. Let them clear the table and wash the dishes. I'd had enough.

"Jen," Dad called after me, but I heard Moura say, "Let her go sulk in her room if that's what she wishes."

"But this isn't like her," Dad began. "Normally she—"

I didn't wait to hear what I normally did or didn't do. "Normal" was how I'd acted before Moura came. "Normal" was Dad and me. Couldn't he understand that?

With Tink bounding ahead, I fled to my room. Kieryn was still in cat shape, sound asleep on my bed. She opened her eyes and watched as I flung myself down beside her.

"Where's my food?" she asked. "That good stuff ye promised me?"

"Just because you're a cat doesn't mean you have to act like one," I said. "Always thinking about food, just like Tink. Can't you see I'm upset?"

Kieryn twitched her tail in annoyance. "All I've had today is half a bowl of milk. Skimmed, at that. Wouldn't ye be hungry, too?"

I sighed and turned my head away from the cat's probing eyes. "Of course I'd be hungry," I said. "But I couldn't stand sitting at that table another minute." I reached out and stroked Kieryn's head. "I'll sneak down and raid the refrigerator later. I promise."

Somewhat placated, Kieryn moved closer. "How did things go down below?"

"Nobody said a word to me, not even 'pass the butter.' They talked and talked, mostly about movies and books and music. Then Dad finally looked at me. Do you know what he said?"

Kieryn pondered a moment. "Most likely he told ye to clear the table."

"How did you know?"

"A lucky guess." Kieryn snuggled closer. "And ye came upstairs without a morsel for me."

"Yes."

"That was foolish of ye."

"What do you mean?"

"Ye left yer daddy alone with *her.* Every time ye look bad, *her* looks better. Ye're digging yer own grave, ye dimbob."

I cradled my head in my arms. Kieryn was right. I'd made a mistake. "Should I go down and apologize?"

"It might help." Kieryn stuck her rump up in the air and stretched her front legs, just like a real cat. "And don't forget my dinner this time," she added.

I washed my face and went slowly downstairs. Cadoc raised his head and narrowed his eyes at the sight of me, but Dad and Moura were too interested in each other to notice my presence. Cadoc rose to his feet and walked slowly toward me. Terrified, I stood still and let him sniff my clothes.

Moura noticed the dog and laughed. "He must smell cat on you, Jen. Wouldn't it be wonderful to have a nose like his? Think of the secrets it tells him."

"Please call him," I asked her. "He makes me nervous."

"Nonsense. Cadoc's a darling." Nonetheless, she did as I asked, and Cadoc left me reluctantly. To him I was a half-read book, and he wanted to know the ending.

I walked over to my father and put my arms around his neck. "I'm sorry I was rude, Dad."

He kissed my cheek. "It's all right. We left some cake for you. It's double chocolate with raspberry sauce, your favorite."

Avoiding Moura's eyes, I gathered plates and silverware and cleared the table. A few minutes later, while I was washing the dishes, I heard Dad say, "Your room is in the east wing. It has a lovely view of the woods and its own little sitting room and bath. You should be very comfortable."

"I'm sure it will be perfect, Hugh."

"Shall I help you carry your bags?"

Moura must have nodded because I heard them both climbing the stairs to the second floor. Cadoc's toenails clicked on the steps behind them.

In their absence, I filled a plastic bag with leftovers, as well as enough chocolate cake for two. Safely back in my room, I locked my door and spread out the feast for Kieryn. She changed into a girl again.

"This is just like a slumber party," I said, thinking about my old friends back home and the good times we had sleeping over at each other's houses.

Kieryn looked at me, obviously puzzled. "Slumber party? How can ye have a party if everyone's asleep?"

"Oh, we talk in our sleep and walk in our sleep. Why, we even dance and play games and eat in our sleep." I sat back to see if she believed me. It was hard to imagine not knowing what a slumber party was, and I couldn't help teasing her.

Kieryn narrowed her strange green eyes. "I think ye're jesting," she said.

"Sorry. I guess you don't have slumber parties in your world."

Kieryn shook her head. "Are they fun?"

I nodded. "We stay at each other's houses all night, and the whole point is *not* to sleep. We all try to be the one who stays awake longest. We eat and play games and watch scary movies."

"Movies?"

I explained movies. At first Kieryn thought I was teasing her again, but I finally convinced her. "Back home, I had a television in my room, but TVs don't work here unless you have a satellite dish. And Dad hasn't gotten around to that. He says we'll do just fine without TV."

Kieryn was totally bewildered by now, so I had to explain TV and satellite dishes and all sorts of things I didn't really know much about.

"Your world must be very old-fashioned," I finally said.

Kieryn shrugged. "We have magic. We don't need anything else."

I didn't have an answer to that, so I changed the subject. "Did you like the chocolate cake?"

"Scrumptidy-licious, the best cake ever." Kieryn licked the icing from her fingers and smiled. "Yer father is indeed a marvel."

"Just so he stays that way," I grumbled. "Who knows what Moura will do to him?"

Just as I spoke, I heard Dad's footsteps in the hall. "Who are you talking to, Jen?"

"The cats," I said.

Dad turned the knob. "Can I come in to say good night?"

In a flash, Kieryn vanished and a little gray cat sat beside me, licking chocolate from its paws.

"Sure," I called.

"The door's locked."

I jumped up and turned the key. "Sorry. I just wanted to be sure Cadoc couldn't get in here."

Dad shook his head. "Cadoc is superintelligent, but I've never heard of a dog opening a door."

Dad looked past me at the remnants of my feast. "How often have I told you not to feed Tink leftovers? And you'll never teach Mist to eat cat food if you feed her table scraps."

"Sorry. She was just so hungry." I scooped up the cat and cuddled her till she rumbled with purrs.

Dad sighed. "Now, go brush your teeth and take a bath. Then into bed with you!"

"Yes, sir!"

Dad hesitated in the doorway. "Please try to treat Moura with respect. You know she'll be my wife soon."

His words shattered my good mood. "Oh, Dad, don't marry that woman. Please, please, *please* don't. Can't you see what she's really like?"

Dad frowned. "Jen, it's late and I'm tired. I just can't talk about this right now." He backed out of my room and closed the door behind him.

Still holding Kieryn, I sank down on my bed. Dad simply would not listen to a word against Moura. Even worse, she and her hateful dog were in our house, sleeping here every night. In the guise of taking inventory, they'd soon be poking their sharp noses into every room, including mine. How long could I keep Kieryn's true nature a secret?

Kieryn stirred in my arms. "I know ye're a wee bit cross, and maybe upset as well, but a bath would be a treat. Hot water, soap. It's been a long, dirty time since I've had me a good wash."

Wearily, I headed for the bathroom carrying Kieryn. A bath . . . all I wanted was to get in bed and sleep for a hundred years.

STILL IN HER CAT body, Kieryn perched on the edge of the tub and watched me turn on the hot water. "Do ye have sweet-smelling bath salts?" she asked. "I'd so love a long soak to wash off the grime. It were dirty in that globe, ye know. Dust to make ye sneeze your head clean off."

Obediently, I produced what she wanted and added it to the water. The steamy air filled with the sweet scent of my favorite bath foam, a Christmas present from my best friend, Janie.

Kieryn jumped into the water and became a girl again, her body hidden in bubbles. "Lovely," she sighed. "Absolutely lovely."

I watched her sink down to wet her hair. Her black curls spread in the water, framing her little pointed face. She closed her eyes and smiled. "Ye cannot imagine how good hot water feels."

After that, she had nothing to say. She splashed in the tub like a child, splattering water everywhere. Floors, walls, even me. She laughed and I laughed, too. For the first time in a long while, I let myself have fun.

It didn't last long. Someone pounded on the bathroom door, and I heard Dad shout, "Jen, what on earth are you doing in there?"

Instantly, Kieryn transformed herself into Mist. Bad decision. She began swimming in the tub, her eyes wide with fear. Quickly I lifted her out and wrapped her in a towel.

When I opened the door, Dad and Moura stood in the hall, staring at me. His face was bewildered, hers expressionless. "I was giving Mist a bath," I said.

"How did you get so much water on the floor?" Dad asked.

I shrugged. "Mist didn't like being in the tub."

"Cats don't need baths," Moura observed. "They clean themselves."

"Well, she'd been in the woods, and she was dirty," I muttered. "I thought she'd like a bath."

Dad sighed. "I suggest you clean up the bathroom and go to bed."

"And put the cats outside," Moura added. "Like all nocturnal animals, they hunt by night."

I held Kieryn so tightly she mewed. "Tink sleeps on my bed, and Mist will, too."

Moura glanced at Dad, hoping he'd back her up. To her obvious disappointment, he sided with me. "Jen's lonely at night," he explained. "Having Tink close by comforts her. And Mist's too small to leave outside in the dark."

"Don't be silly." Moura frowned at Kieryn. "That cat was living in the woods when Jen found her."

"Moura," Dad said gently, "if it makes her feel better, why shouldn't Jen keep the cats in her room? I see no harm in it."

Moura shrugged. "Do as you wish. Jen is your daughter. You know her far better than I do." Her voice was sweet and light, and she smiled at Dad to show him he'd convinced her.

Dad put his arm around her shoulders, pleased to see she wasn't cross with him. He put his other arm around me and drew me close for a good-night kiss. Once again the musky smell of Moura's perfume filled my nostrils. Fine cobweb strands of her black hair brushed my face. In my arms, Kieryn shrank down as small as she could. I wouldn't have been surprised if she'd changed herself into a mouse. But, of course, she couldn't do that without giving herself away.

I gave Dad a tight one-armed hug, nearly squashing Kieryn in the process, and went to my room. Safe behind my locked door, I put Kieryn on the bed, changed into my pajamas, and climbed in beside her.

"That was scary," I whispered. "The way Moura was looking at me, almost as if she knew—"

"Ah, *her*'s a witchy old thing, *her* is. *Her* knows something's going on, but she don't know what, and that drives her dafty." Kieryn shivered and snuggled closer. "Ye be careful, Jen. *Her*'s a tricksy one."

The next morning, I left Kieryn dozing on my windowsill. The sunlight glistened on her sweet, clean fur. Her sides rose and fell, and she purred softly, content to stay where she was and wait for me to bring her breakfast. Tink chose to follow me down to the kitchen.

Moura sat at the table, drinking a cup of coffee. Today she'd braided her long hair into one thick black rope. She wore black jeans and a long-sleeved black T-shirt that made her look even slimmer. The red stone in her pendant caught the morning sunlight and sent reflections bouncing over the wall and ceiling whenever she moved.

"Where's Dad?" I picked up the bowl of cereal and glass of orange juice he'd left on the counter for me.

"He's gone to Mingo to pick up a few things at the hardware store. I've encouraged him to work on the garden behind the house. Your uncle had a way with flowers and herbs."

She paused and waited for me to join her at the table. When I hesitated, she smiled. "Come and sit beside me. I don't eat little girls, you know."

Held by her eyes, I sat down reluctantly and began to eat my cereal.

"I'm so happy to have this opportunity to talk to you, Jen." Moura eyed me over the rim of her coffee cup. The sun lit blue highlights in her hair, almost as iridescent as a starling's feathers. The house was silent except for the ticking of the clock and the hum of the refrigerator. By Moura's side, Cadoc sat still as a statue, and Tink huddled by my feet.

I met Moura's eyes briefly but said nothing. Outside, on the windowsill, a robin strutted up and down, cocking its head at us now and then.

"May I tell you a story?" she asked.

I shrugged. The only way to escape the story was to leave the kitchen, but for some reason I couldn't summon the energy to excuse myself.

"Once upon a time, people believed the woods behind this house were enchanted," she began in that soft, musical voice of hers. "Rumors abounded of entrances to other worlds. Magic worlds. Fairyland, perhaps. Believers traveled from great distances to explore the paths and rivers. Some disappeared, never to be seen again. Others searched without success. Frustrated and angry, they denounced the stories as lies."

Moura paused, but I said nothing. I continued to eat my cereal as if I took no interest in her story.

"Your great-uncle built his house here because of the stories. He had a deep interest in the occult, as his tower indicates. All his life he sought the entrance to that other world. He never found it. But he did find something else."

Once again, Moura paused to gauge my reaction. Without looking at her, I nodded. "Dad said Uncle Thaddeus was eccentric."

"That's not the word I would choose," Moura said softly. "Thaddeus Mostyn had a brilliant mind. A unique curiosity."

Unwillingly, I looked across the table at her. The sun struck her face, emphasizing its beauty but at the same time revealing tiny lines in her pale skin, like fine cracks beneath the surface of old china.

"Don't you want to know what your great-uncle found—and trapped?" Moura asked, her voice low.

I already knew, but I was curious to hear what Moura would say. Hoping to show my indifference, I shrugged and answered, "I guess so."

"You recall my desire to find the witch catcher?"

"Yes."

"And my dismay when I found your cat had broken it?"

"Yes."

"Do you remember what I told you?"

"You said I was in danger."

She nodded and poured herself another cup of coffee. "But I didn't tell you why."

"No." I poured myself a cup of coffee and added sugar and cream. Moura raised one fine black eyebrow but said nothing.

She leaned toward me, her body thin and angular. "When the glass is broken, the evil spirit finds someone foolish enough to help it." She paused and looked at me sharply. "It will do anything to find its own kind."

Moura's intensity made me uneasy. I drew back from her, glad to feel Tink leap into my lap and begin to purr as if he were telling me something. If only Kieryn had given me the gift to understand cats, I might have known what it was. At the open window, the robin chirped. Moura glanced at it, and it flew away.

"I told you my grandmother knew your uncle," Moura

went on. "She was a curious woman. When she found the witch trap hanging in the tower, she took it down and studied it . . . peered through the glass, pressed her ear against it. She saw something inside, heard it begging to be released, but she knew better than to listen. She put the ball back where she'd found it."

Liar, I thought. It wasn't your grandmother who knew Uncle Thaddeus—it was you. *You* gave him the traps. *You* wanted what he caught.

Moura leaned across the table and tilted my chin up, forcing me to look at her. "You seem bored, Jen. Doesn't my story interest you?"

"Not especially." I tried to look away, but her pale eyes held mine for a moment, probing as if she hoped to read my mind. It was a relief to turn my head, to break away from her gaze.

"Do you wish me to continue?"

I shrugged. "If you want." Instead of looking at her, I watched a fly walk across the ceiling.

Moura went on with her lies. "My grandmother never had the opportunity to return to the tower. When your uncle realized she was interested in the witch trap, he locked her out."

He *sealed* you out, I thought, with those runes on the door. He knew what you were. He knew what you were after.

"You saw your uncle's paintings," Moura continued, "the strange creature trapped behind glass, her hands pressed against her prison walls, her mouth open in a plea for freedom. Thaddeus Mostyn painted her over and over again, never satisfied with his renderings. Always beginning again."

She paused to swat at the fly, now crawling around the sugar bowl. Off it flew.

"And then one evening," Moura said softly, "Thaddeus Mostyn suffered apoplexy—a stroke, you'd call it. He never recovered his ability to speak or to walk. He could no longer go to the tower."

Yes, I thought, yes—I know all about that stroke. And who caused it. Witch. Liar. I hate you.

Keeping my face as expressionless as Moura's, I said, "And the globe was left there with the girl trapped inside."

"Not a girl," she said. "A demon from another world, untrustworthy, dangerous, wicked, a teller of lies, a deceiver."

The fly buzzed over her head. Annoyed, Moura picked up the newspaper and tried to kill it. Again she missed. "Filthy creature," she muttered. "Full of germs."

To keep from looking at Moura, I picked up my cup and stared into my coffee. "If something wicked was inside that globe, why did you and Mr. Ashbourne want it so badly?" I ventured.

"To make certain it didn't fall into the wrong hands. Mr. Ashbourne collects witch catchers to prevent the accidental release of the evil beings trapped within."

Suddenly, Moura laid her hand on mine. "Now do you understand why you must tell me everything you know about the globe, Jen? You mustn't put yourself in peril because of your innocence." She paused, her eyes locked on mine again. "Or should we say your ignorance? Your stubbornness? Call it what we will, but you are endangering yourself."

I pulled my hand away. "Tink broke the globe. There was nothing but broken glass in my closet." This was true, so I looked her in the eye while I spoke. "You saw it yourself. Shards of glass all over the floor."

"Ah, but perhaps you encountered the creature later," Moura persisted. "In the woods, maybe. Foolish child! You could be enchanted without even knowing it. You have no idea what you've gotten yourself into."

Although I knew better than to believe Moura, her words scared me, awoke possibilities that hadn't occurred to me. Doubts. I'd believed Kieryn almost from the beginning. Had I been too trusting? All of this was new to me—magic, witchcraft, fairyland, spells, traps.

Moura got up and came around the table. She hugged me. Her perfume surrounded me as dense as a cloud of smoke. I felt dizzy, woozy, breathless. Moura loved me. . . . She wanted to protect me from danger . . . from Kieryn. I relaxed in her arms, I breathed in her perfume, filling my lungs with it as if I'd been drowning in ordinary air.

"My dear, dear child," Moura whispered, her breath cool in my ear. "Allow me to be a mother to you, let me keep you from danger and harm."

"A mother," I murmured. "I had a mother, a lovely mother, but she died, she . . ."

"Yes, yes." Moura soothed me. "I cannot replace her, but I can love you as you need to be loved. You can confide in me. Your secrets will be safe with me. Your joys, your sorrows. Let me into your heart, darling Jen."

Helpless, I opened my heart, and Moura sank into it. I loved her. She loved me. Safe. I felt so safe. I opened my eyes and gazed into her beautiful face. In my lap, Tink growled. He dug his claws into my legs and lashed his tail, but I ignored him.

"Oh, Moura, oh, Mother." I took a deep breath, eager to win her love, to be her daughter.

12

JUST AS I WAS about to tell Moura everything she wanted to know, Dad opened the kitchen door. A gust of fresh air came in with him and dissipated Moura's heavy musk of perfume.

"Well, well," Dad said, "what a nice surprise to find you two so friendly."

As the bittersweet scent faded, I shook my head and took a deep breath. My dizziness vanished, and I pulled away from Moura.

Her body tensed with fury, but she let me go. Forcing herself to smile, she greeted Dad pleasantly. "I believe we're making some progress." She hugged Dad. He couldn't see the anger and frustration in her face, but I could.

I thanked Dad silently with all my heart for choosing that moment to return. Moura had led me into her trap so quickly, so easily. I was indeed a foolish child.

"What did you purchase for the garden?" Moura asked.

"A spade, a rake, and a hoe to start with," Dad said.

"How about the plants I suggested?"

He pulled out a list and read, "Foxglove, deadly nightshade, lobelia, monkshood, bleeding heart." He looked at

Moura. "I must say, the cashier seemed perplexed by my choices. She says they're all poisonous."

Moura smiled and shrugged. "One man's flower is another man's poison."

I shuddered, but Dad slid into a chair beside me, eager for the coffee Moura poured for him.

Ignoring me, he said to Moura, "I've been thinking about Mr. Ashbourne. He was a good sport about the witch catcher. Maybe I should sell Uncle Thaddeus's paintings to him. They aren't to my taste. Why shouldn't they go to someone who appreciates them?"

"I'm sure Ciril will be delighted," Moura said. "Shall I call him to make an appointment?"

"Why not this afternoon?" Dad asked.

"Fine." With a smile for both of us, Moura left the table to go call Mr. Ashbourne.

Dad watched her leave the room. "Lovely woman," he said softly. "I was so pleased to see you two together. I knew you'd grow to love her as much as I do."

Wordlessly, I pushed my chair back from the table and left Dad to drink his coffee alone. What was the sense of telling him nothing had changed between Moura and me? In fact, I detested her more than ever. Worse yet, I was also scared of her.

With Tink at my heels, I rushed upstairs but paused at the top. How could I face Kieryn? I'd almost betrayed her.

Tink rubbed against my legs and purred, then ran to my closed door and looked at me. "Mew, mew," he cried, almost as if he were telling me it was all right. Kieryn would forgive me.

Still ashamed, I opened my door and saw Kieryn-the-cat sitting in the middle of my bed, washing her face with her paw. She watched me cross the room and sink down beside her.

"Ye needn't tell me. I know what *her* almost done." Kieryn went on grooming herself. "I be a cat now, but I were the bird at the window and the fly on the wall. I be full of tricksy tricks."

I glanced at the gray cat and smiled. No matter what shape she took—fairy, cat, bird, or fly—Kieryn was my friend. How could I have let Moura fill my head with doubts?

"I thought I could outsmart that witch," I muttered, "and look what happened. How could I have been so stupid?"

"Ye're wiser now, ain't ye?" Kieryn asked. "*Her* won't find it so easy to trick ye again."

I rubbed the cat's furry head. "I hope you're right."

We lay on the bed, side by side, watching the dance of leaf shadows on the wall. After a while, Kieryn stretched and took her own form. Her hair, clean and silky from her bath last night, curled around her face in dark tendrils. She was more beautiful than I'd realized. An exotic creature with pale green skin, slanted eyes, and a pointed chin, not like any race on earth.

She sat up suddenly and peered down at me. "I'm all of a fret about my brother, Brynn, Jen. Him and the aunties been in them traps a fierce long time. Years and years, I reckon."

"Do you think Moura has the traps in her shop?"

Kieryn shook her head. "They be with *him*, the collector, I'm most certain of it."

"Mr. Ashbourne's coming here this very afternoon," I said, "to buy Uncle Thaddeus's paintings."

"The ones the old skitch done of me when I were trapped and helpless?"

"Mr. Ashbourne told Dad he's interested in the fairy world."

Kieryn looked fierce. "*Him* interested in the fairy world," she muttered. "All *him* wants is to bring it to ruin, *him* and *her* both, so their kinkind can rule it. Dark and evil *them* be." She spit on her thumb and drew a circle in the air. "Wicked to wicked, bad to bad, dark to dark."

"Is that a curse?" My heart bumped for a second like a car on a rutted road.

"Aye." Kieryn gave me a sly look. "But it's no more than a boshy mosquito bite to ones like *them*. If Mam were here, she'd do up a big whopping curse that would set *them* back a bit, I can tell ye that. She has the power, Mam does."

"Do you know where Mr. Ashbourne lives?" I asked.

Kieryn grinned. "Nay, but when he comes here for the paintings, we can hide ourselves in his car and let the old snark drive us right to his house—like as if he was our own private chauffeur."

She threw back her head and laughed, but I didn't join her—Mr. Ashbourne scared me even more than Moura.

"But what if he catches us?" I asked.

"Ah, don't fash yerself, Jen. Haven't ye noticed I be a tricksy girl?"

"Yes, but they're tricksy, too. Don't forget, they caught you once. How do you know they won't—"

"Choky sumac and hemlock juice, ye're such a timmy-tim." Kieryn threw herself back on the bed so hard the mattress bounced. "Go with me or stay here like a baby tittot bird—see if I cares."

Dad saved me from answering Kieryn by hollering that lunch was ready. I left her curled up in a cross gray ball on my bed and trudged slowly downstairs to sit through another stiff, unpleasant meal with Moura and Dad. As usual, the two of them chattered away about books and poetry and music while I sat silently nibbling a tuna fish sandwich that tasted like sawdust.

Just as I got up to clear the table, the doorbell rang. "Will you get that, Jen?" Dad asked.

Cadoc beat me to the door, nose on alert, tail wagging. Mr. Ashbourne stood on the threshold, dressed in a tweed jacket and corduroy slacks, a paisley ascot tucked into his shirt collar. The perfect gentleman—unless you knew what I knew.

I stepped aside to let him in. Giving me a brief glance of dislike, he strode into the hall and shook hands with Dad. While he and Dad talked, I noticed Kieryn-the-cat on the stairs. She'd fixed her attention on Cadoc, who seemed to be equally interested in her. When the dog rose to his feet and began moving stealthily toward the kitten, I darted across the room and scooped her up. Cadoc stared at me, his pale eyes scary. With a low growl, he retreated to Moura's side.

"He doesn't care for cats." Moura rested her elegant hand on Cadoc's head. "And neither do I. Sneaky creatures that can't be trusted—rather like children."

Dad was too involved with Mr. Ashbourne and the paintings to hear what Moura had said. I looked at her but kept silent. I was sure she disliked children as much as she disliked cats.

In a louder voice, she said, "Hugh, we forgot to take that cat to the vet. Perhaps this afternoon? I'd hate to see it contaminate Tink with some dreadful feline disease."

Mr. Ashbourne glanced at Kieryn and me and frowned. "Cats," he muttered. "Don't see why anyone tolerates having the beasts in their homes."

"Get me out of here," Kieryn whispered in my ear. "*Her* and *him*'s thinking evil thoughts about both me and ye. And so's her hound."

Anxious to escape Mr. Ashbourne, Moura, and Cadoc, I told Dad I was going outside to play.

"Stay close to the house, Jen," he said, his attention focused on Mr. Ashbourne.

Mr. Ashbourne's shiny black van sat in the shade of a maple tree. The side door was open, waiting to be loaded with paintings.

Kieryn leapt from my arms and darted into the van. "Quick, Jen—get in afore *him* sees us."

I ran to the door and poked my head inside. "Are you sure this is a good idea?"

"'Tis the one way I know to go to *his* house," she said.

"But—"

"Get in," Kieryn insisted. "Ye promised ye'd help me rescue Brynn."

"I know but—"

"Fie fie fiddlesticks on you," Kieryn said with a hiss. "I reckon I'll go it alone, then. Mam always said ye can't trust a human to keep a promise."

I reached into the van to pull her out, but she scurried to the very back and regarded me with angry eyes, her tail puffed to double its size.

"Please, Kieryn," I begged. "He's a bad man."

"Don't ye think I know that already, ye dimbob, timtim promise breaker?"

I didn't want to get in that van, but it was clear nothing would change Kieryn's mind. With me or without me, she meant to go to Mr. Ashbourne's house and rescue her kin. How could I let her go all by herself?

While I stood there hesitating, I heard Dad say, "You take one end, Ciril, and I'll take the other."

They were coming with the paintings. In a few seconds, it would be too late to go with Kieryn. Trying not to think of what might happen, I climbed quickly into the back of the van. A pile of packing quilts lay on the floor. I chose one for a cover and curled into the smallest ball possible. Kieryn crouched beside me, her green cat eyes aglow with watchfulness as Dad and Mr. Ashbourne approached the van.

13

"LOAD THEM IN BACK," Mr. Ashbourne said in his suave English voice.

I heard Dad put the paintings in the back seat carefully, one at a time, breathing hard as he wrestled with them.

"Where did Jen run off to?" Moura asked.

"She can't have gone far," Dad said. "I told her to stay close to the house."

"Thanks, Hugh," Mr. Ashbourne said, obviously unconcerned with my whereabouts. "Your uncle's paintings will have a good home. And don't forget the books you mentioned. I'd like to go up to the tower and take a look at them one day soon."

The van door slid shut. We felt the tilt of Mr. Ashbourne's weight as he settled himself behind the wheel.

"Good afternoon," he called to Dad and Moura. "I'll be in touch."

When the van moved forward, my stomach lurched. If only I were dreaming this. I couldn't remember ever being more scared or feeling so helpless.

Mr. Ashbourne turned on the radio and hummed along with a piece by Mozart that I'd once played when I was taking flute lessons. Beside me Kieryn lay still, as tense as Tink when he was about to pounce on something.

We rode up hill and down, along a winding road, stopping perhaps forty-five minutes later. Mr. Ashbourne got out of the van and opened the sliding door. One by one, he began removing the paintings.

"May I help, sir?" a man asked.

"Yes, take these to the drawing room, Simkins."

"Yes, sir."

The men's footsteps crunched on gravel as they walked away. Cautiously, Kieryn crept out from under the packing quilt and peered through the van's rear window.

"It be a big tall mansion of a house," she whispered, "with towers and all and more chimneys than I ever did see, made of pinky orange brick all covered with ivy. Grand. *Him*'s rich as a king in this world, *him* is, on the fairy gold he stole."

"Have they both gone inside the house?" My legs ached from being curled up so long, and I yearned to have a good stretch.

"Aye, and taken Mostyn's paintings with them, the boshy pair. What do *him* want with my portrait?"

"Who's the other man?"

Kieryn hissed in contempt. "I reckon they found him in yer world and won him over with pisky lies and promises."

Cautiously, I poked my head out from under the blanket, but I didn't dare join Kieryn at the window. "What should we do now?"

"Wait till dark and sneak inside. We'll search the place till we finds them snarky traps."

"What if Mr. Ashbourne has a dog like Cadoc?"

Kieryn twitched her tail. "I gave the van a right good sniff. Not a stinky whiff of hound anywhere."

She crawled under the packing quilt and curled up. "We might as well sleep a while to pass the time till night."

Unfortunately, it wasn't as easy for me to nap as it was for Kieryn. In cat form she was a natural sleeper. Not me. I imagined dogs or even wolves creeping around the van, sniffing me out. I worried about Dad, standing at the door, calling my name over and over again. I pictured Moura close beside him, telling him not to worry, engulfing him in her perfume, fogging his thoughts until he forgot all about me.

The sun sank lower, the shadows stretched longer. Birds stopped singing. Crickets and cicadas took their place, shrill and insistent. A breeze sprang up. The blue sky faded to pale violet and then gray. At last, darkness blurred the treetops and lights appeared in the mansion's windows.

Cautiously, I slid the van's door open and got out. Kieryn slunk across the lawn and I followed. The moon had begun to rise, so we stuck to the shadows.

"How will we get inside?" I whispered.

Kieryn paused in the bushes by the back door and looked at me. "Supposing I magic ye into a cat?"

If I hadn't been so scared, I would have laughed. "Me, a cat? That's impossible. You can't do it."

Kieryn narrowed her eyes and twitched her tail. "Even with Mostyn's blood in yer veins, I doubt ye can shape-change on yer own, but if ye do what I say, I reckon ye'll be a cat afore ye know it."

She rubbed against my legs. "Put yer hand on my head. Stroke me all over the way I done Tink. Think hard about cats. How they look and act and sound. What they eat. The shape of them and the feel of them. The sound of them, the smell of them. Their paws and claws and whiskers. Their long tails and rough tongues. Think of cats, cats, *cats* with all yer heart and head, and feel ye're one with them. With me."

"I'm scared," I whispered. "What if something goes wrong? What if you can't change me back?"

"There's much worser things than being a cat for the rest of yer life." Kieryn twitched her tail impatiently. "Brynn's in yon house, trapped in a skitzy ball, and so are my aunties. Do what I tell ye, and ye'll be a lovelier than lovely yellow cat, just like Tink."

Reluctantly, I put my hand on Kieryn's head and closed my eyes. I thought with all my might. Suddenly, I felt every bone transform itself. My muscles knotted and cramped. In a burst of pain, sharp claws shot out of my fingers and toes. Whiskers pricked through my cheeks. Fur grew out of my skin, covering every bit of bare flesh.

When the pain ended, I was a cat as soft and yellow as Tink. I opened my mouth and meowed. I breathed in smells I'd never smelled before. I saw shapes in the dark that usually vanished with daylight. I turned to Kieryn, frightened and excited at the same moment.

"I'm a cat," I whispered. "Look, I even have a tail! But I still feel like a girl."

"Don't worry," Kieryn said. "Before ye know it, ye'll be acting as cattish as cattish can be."

With me staggering behind her, drunk on the night's smells, Kieryn scampered up the steps to the house's back door. It was open to let in the cool night air. Without hesitating, Kieryn pranced into the kitchen and rubbed against a pair of fat sturdy legs. She purred loudly.

A huge woman stared down at Kieryn and me. I'd never realized what humans looked like to cats. To Tink, I must be gigantic. But, I hoped, not as fearsome as this woman.

"What do you think you're doing in here?" With a sudden lunge, the woman grabbed for Kieryn. Missing her, she went for me.

In my newborn cat state, I was an easy target. Seizing me by the nape of my furry little neck, she dangled me in front of her big red face. This close, I could see a scattering of coarse black hairs on her upper lip and more sprouting from her nostrils; big yellow teeth, one capped with gold; a mole on her cheek. Her shaggy eyebrows lowered in a frown above her small eyes. "Mr. Ashbourne hates cats!" she yelled.

While the woman ranted, Kieryn crept up behind her and sunk her teeth and claws into the woman's leg. With a scream of surprise, my capturer flung me across the kitchen with such force I hit the wall and slid to the floor.

"Run!" Kieryn yowled. "Run!"

My head ached, but I tore after her. With the woman in noisy pursuit, we raced up a narrow flight of stairs, down a hall, into a room, and under a bed. We saw the woman charge past the open door without looking into the room. "Cats!" she shrieked. "Cats in the house!"

Suddenly, Kieryn shrank, smaller and smaller, until she was a tiny furry creature with whiskers, a skinny tail, and dainty pink paws. A mouse—a live toy, a delicate morsel, a cat's delight. I reached out with my claws and caught her.

"Ninny bob!" Kieryn squeaked. "Don't eat me. Change yerself!"

Horrified, I let her go. "Sorry," I whispered. "Sorry. I forgot who I am."

"Think mice," Kieryn whispered. "Think hard, as hard as you can!"

I shut my eyes and put my mind into mouse gear. How they looked, what they ate, how they acted. I remembered the pair of white mice in my kindergarten classroom standing on their hind legs to drink from their water bottle, tiny sharp teeth, twitchy noses, pink feet. Then, with a familiar flash of pain, I shrank into a small, furry body.

"Oh, good on ye, Jen," Kieryn squeaked. Whiskers twitching, she led me through a small hole and into safety between the walls of the house.

Beyond the thick plaster, we heard Mr. Ashbourne, Simkins, and the cook, whose name seemed to be Rose, running up and down the hall, searching the rooms, peering under beds, and finding nothing—of course.

"Rose must've had a nip of the cooking sherry," Simkins grumbled. "For there ain't a sign of a cat anywhere I can see."

"I ain't drunk a drop of nothing but coffee all day," Rose protested. "I seen those cats, and I got the scratches to prove it."

"Well, my dear friends," Mr. Ashbourne said in his lovely voice, "we've searched every conceivable feline hiding place. If the odious creatures were indeed in this house, they must have run out a door or jumped from a window."

"Too bad Cadoc ain't here," Simkins added. "I never seen a cat that could escape that dog."

Their footsteps and voices faded as they trudged downstairs. Kieryn and I fixed our beady black eyes on each other. We would have sighed in relief if we hadn't been mice.

"Can we change back to cats now?" I asked hopefully. "I don't like being so small."

"Not yet. We be safer this way." Kieryn turned and headed down the tunnel. "Let's see where this goes."

We hadn't gone far when she stopped me. "Shh! There's mice up ahead."

At first all I heard was chittering and chattering and squeaking, but the longer I listened, the more I understood.

The mice were talking to each other—about Kieryn and me.

"Two strangers in tunnel five," one was saying.

"Big'uns hunt 'em."

"They hide."

"Afeared."

"Should we be helping?"

Silence. Little scribbles and scrabbles, pitters and patters.

After a while, one said, "I be scared of strangers."

"They smell funny," another said. "Not quite right."

"Cat whiff."

"Big'un whiff."

Kieryn nudged me forward. "Let's talk to 'em."

Cautiously, I crept around a curve behind Kieryn. Ahead was a mouse-sized room packed with dozens of mice—dainty pink paws, beady black eyes, long tails. They bunched together and watched Kieryn and me approach.

An elderly mouse came forward, pushed by those behind him, and regarded us with shiny eyes. "Who you?" His voice shook a little. "Whyfor you come to House of Ashbourne?"

Kieryn stepped ahead. The mice moved back, their noses wrinkled in disgust. "Cat whiff," one whispered. "Big'un whiff," another muttered.

"Most honorable Thane of Ashbourne," Kieryn began. "It's true we stink of cat and big'un. We mean ye no harm, and we most humbly apologize for our bad whiff."

The thane waved his hand as if our smell were not important. "Whyfor here?" he asked again.

"*Him* is my foe," Kieryn replied. "*Him* keeps my brother, Brynn, and my aunties in traps. I've come to take them home. Do ye know where *him* hides the traps?"

The mice pressed together, whispering in high voices and staring at Kieryn and me. I still couldn't understand them completely—too many were squeaking at once—but I caught words like "witch," "spells," "evil," "magic," "shape changer," "*him*," "Ashbourne," and so on. I moved a little closer to Kieryn. "What are they saying?"

"Aw, they be mushy-headed timtimmies," Kieryn whispered. "They're afeared I'll change back to cat shape and gobble 'em up. Pish on 'em. I should do it. Serve 'em right."

Finally, the thane spoke. "Tell how traps look."

"They be skitzy glass globes, all pretty with color," Kieryn said. "They hang on long shiny silver chains. Maybe from beams in the ceiling. Maybe in a window. Turn and twist, turn and twist, like fire in sunlight and ice in moonlight. Magic, they be. Bad magic."

The squeaking began again. A little mouse darted forward and tugged at the thane's tail. The thane listened to his high piping voice and then turned to Kieryn and me.

"Short Tail knows where traps be. Promise no harm to him and he take you there."

Kieryn and I made a solemn promise which involved kissing the thane's paw and walking around him three times with our eyes closed. When the thane raised his paw in dismissal, Short Tail raced into a tunnel. Kieryn and I scampered after him.

The tunnel turned upward through the walls, steep, narrow, hard to climb. When we finally reached the top, all three of us sprawled on our bellies, too exhausted to say a word.

Short Tail recovered first. "Not many come up here," he told us. "No food. But good window for looking out. See far. Sky, clouds, treetops. Higher than birds fly."

"Where be the traps?" Kieryn asked. She spoke with her head down—fearful, I guessed, of being sucked inside another globe.

"This way." Short Tail led us out of the tunnel and into a large room. "There." He pointed upward. A globe like the one I'd found in the tower hung in a tall window, slowly revolving in the night breeze. Others hung from rafters above our heads, dozens of them, glittering and glowing, swaying in the moonlight, clinking together now and then, beautiful beyond words.

Without looking up, Kieryn whispered, "Be it true, Jen? Do ye see a trap?"

"Lots of them. Keep your eyes closed."

Short Tail stared at Kieryn. "The thane were right. You be a witch." He backed away uneasily.

Kieryn ignored the mouse. "Ye must break 'em, Jen. Every last one."

"I can't. I'm too small to reach them."

"Think yerself back to yer true self, ye great twit," Kieryn said. "Ye don't want to stay a mousie, do ye?"

I sniffed and snuffled and rubbed my eyes with my little pink paws. "I don't know how to change back," I whimpered tearfully. "Can't you change first and then hold my hand and help me?"

"Ye know I cannot. With these skitzy globes hanging over me head, I'd soon be trapped again."

"Then tell me how," I begged in a little whiny mouse voice. "I don't think I can do it without you."

Kieryn sighed so loudly that Short Tail retreated to the tunnel's opening, ready to vanish at the first sign of real danger.

"Do what ye did afore ye changed into a cat and then to a mousie," Kieryn said, making an obvious effort to be patient. "Think as hard as ye can about yerself. How ye looked, how ye were. Picture yer old girly self. Feel what ye felt in yer head. See yerself. Be yerself."

I crouched on the floor and thought hard about the girl I'd been just a little while ago. Tall and thin, untidy brown hair, teeth a little too big for my mouth, freckles all over my face, arms, and legs, twelve years old, good at reading, bad at math, a scar on my arm from a bike accident. I concentrated on the image of myself for what seemed like a long time. My head ached with the effort, but nothing happened. My mouse tail still twitched, my little pink feet still gripped the floor, my whiskers still quivered.

Both Kieryn and Short Tail watched, she with angry impatience and he with terror.

At last, I saw my true self—scared and lonely Jen, Jen the shy one, Jen the sad one, left out of games, daydreaming my way through school. With a great flash of pain, I burst out of my mouse skin and sprawled on the floor, a girl again, too exhausted to move.

Short Tail turned and fled into the tunnel. "Big'un!" I heard him cry. "Not mouse. Big'un witchery!"

"Rise ye up, goosey," Kieryn squeaked at me, "and break them traps!"

I got to my feet, dizzy and weak. I felt so big. Huge. A giant. A big'un. Like Alice when she ate from the wrong side of the mushroom. I swayed to the right and then to the left. I was sure I'd hit my head on the rafters. To keep from falling, I leaned against a wall and struggled to find my balance.

Kieryn remained crouched on the floor, her nose on her paws, her eyes shut tight. Over our heads, the globes swayed, touching each other gently. *Clink, clink. Clink, clink.*

"Music it be, their own evil music," Kieryn whispered. "Tempting me. I mustn't look. I mustn't!"

A shaft of moonlight stabbed through the open window. The globes glowed like jewels, casting a shifting pattern of kaleidoscope colors on the floor, on the walls, on me, on Kieryn's furry back. *Clink, clink. Clink, clink.*

"Break 'em!" Kieryn cried to me. "Smash 'em to bits. They be things of evil, full of pain and hurt."

"But they're so beautiful," I protested. "Can't we—"

"No!" Kieryn shouted. "Break all of 'em! Or doom Brynn and me."

Reluctantly I searched the room for something to use, but the globes' colors whirled and swirled around my head, blinding me. The sound they made was like the ringing of tiny silver bells. Dizzy again, I stumbled.

"I can't," I sobbed. "I can't break them."

"You must!" Kieryn cried. "Hit 'em with a chair, a table, a book, ye simple timtimmy. Pull 'em down with yer bare hands and smash 'em on the floor. So many traps make the magic strong. It's pulling at me like magnets pull iron."

With shaking arms, I grabbed a globe and yanked it down. The glass burned my hands, and I threw it against the wall. *Smash.* I reached for another and another. *Smash, crash.* One by one, I hurled them across the room, wild now to destroy them. They burst like bombs, sending colored glass flying. Several exploded with flashes of green light and puffs of smoke. I thought I saw some shapes fly out the window into the night, but I had no idea what I'd freed.

At last, the only globe remaining was the most beautiful of all. It hung by itself in the tall window and turned slowly in the night breeze, its colors glowing in the moonlight.

"There's only one left," I told Kieryn.

"Be quick, be quick!" Kieryn pleaded. "They'll come soon."

I climbed onto the windowsill and reached for the globe. When my fingers brushed the hot glass, it swung away from me, out into the darkness. I teetered, sure I was about to plunge to the ground far below. Somehow I kept my balance and reached for the globe as it swung back toward me. But once again I missed it and barely kept my balance on the windowsill.

Making a huge effort, I grabbed at the globe again, and this time I got it, falling to the floor with it, snapping the chain. The glass shattered and a burst of green light nearly blinded me.

14

A TINY WADDED-UP thing flopped around on the floor, buglike and slimy, the size of a cicada. I drew back, repulsed. My first impulse was to step on it, squash it. But before I had the chance, the creature began to grow and stretch and change. In less than a minute, a boy slightly smaller than Kieryn crouched at my feet, his face greener than hers, his eyes huge with fear.

"Who be ye? Where are my aunties?" he asked, ready to run.

"Brynn!" Kieryn squeaked. "'Tis I, Kieryn! Here on the floor."

Brynn picked up the mouse and cuddled it against his cheek. "Kieryn, I feared ye were lost forever," he whispered. "I never thought to see ye again or to be free of that skitzy globe."

"I'd never desert ye, foolish boy," Kieryn said. "I be yer sister, yer kinkind, truer than true forever and ever."

Brynn looked at me, more suspicious now than fearful. "Who be that? She smells of humankind."

"She be Jen, my true heart friend."

Brynn stared at his sister. "There's nae friendship between our kind and her kind."

Kieryn squirmed away from Brynn and came to me. "That be old-time nonsense, Brynn. It's Jen who freed ye from that skitzy globe. Ye might thank her, ye ungrateful dimbob."

But Brynn wasn't in a mood to thank me. "Where be the aunties?" He looked at me as if I'd done something with them.

"Did ye see them when ye was a-smashing things, Jen?" Kieryn asked.

"There were green flashes all around me, and things flying every which way. Most went out the window."

"Never ye mind," Kieryn said. "The aunties will find us. They was most likely discombobulated."

The noise of footsteps on the stairs startled us. Mr. Ashbourne, Simkins, and the cook were coming, shouting and cursing as they climbed toward us. The very walls seemed to shake with their anger.

"Quick, we must all be mousies," Kieryn cried.

In a flash, Brynn shrank to Kieryn's size, but I froze where I stood, too scared to move, to think, to change my shape. I was a twelve-year-old-girl trapped in a tower room with three enemies rushing closer and closer. How could I be anything else?

"Jen!" Kieryn ran up my leg, her tiny paws tickling my skin. "Think mousie, as I taught ye!"

"I can't," I whispered. "I'm so tired. So tired." It was true. I wanted to lie down on the floor and sleep and then wake up at home in my own bed. I had to be dreaming, had to be. Nothing made sense. I was a girl. How could I become a mouse?

Kieryn perched on my shoulder and peered at me from her jet black eyes. "Ye must! They're almost here."

They were in the hall now, running toward us. In just a few seconds, they'd be at the door, they'd see me.

"Mousie, mousie, mousie," Kieryn chanted. "Long tail, pink feet, soft fur, whiskers, twitchy nose. Be small, be shy. Run and hide from *him*, quick, quick, quick."

"Leave her here," Brynn begged. "Humankind with humankind. Fairykind with fairykind."

"Danger!" Kieryn cried. "*Him* and *her.* Run and hide, mousie, run and hide!"

Hidden in darkness, I saw Ashbourne in the doorway. His scary glasses glowed with a spinning light of their own. "Who's there?" he shouted.

I shut my eyes and shrank from him, shrank small, smaller. Mousie, mousie, mousie. Pain, pressure on all sides, squeezing me into a furry ball. Tail, whiskers, little pink feet. Twitchy nose, shiny black eyes. *Squeak, squeak, squeak*—I ran for the tunnel.

"The mice," Ashbourne cried. "Don't let them get away!"

Feet rushed toward us, stomping, eager to crush us. We zigged and zagged away from them and their big hands.

With Kieryn and Brynn just ahead, I dashed into the tunnel and scurried down through the walls. Behind us, Ashbourne cursed.

Finally, we careened into the mouse meeting hall and stopped, face to face with the thane and several dozen of his subjects.

Short Tail gasped. "Big'uns," he cried, "Witchy big'uns back again!"

The thane held up his paw, his face as stern as a mouse's face can be. "Halt," he commanded. "Explain yourselves."

Kieryn stepped forward. "It be as I told ye," she began, still struggling for breath. "*Him,* who be yer foe as well as ourn, put my brother in a witch trap in the tower." She put out a little pink paw and stroked Brynn's fur. "We came to save him, Jen and me. I used witch magic to make us mousies, small and quick, in and out, no harm to ye or yer kind."

The words "witch magic," flowed through the room, from mouse to frightened mouse. I don't think they even heard the part about no harm.

"No harm!" Kieryn cried again, louder this time. "No harm to ye. Good witch magic."

"Not like Ashbourne?" the thane asked. "Not like Moura?"

"No. They be wicked witches. We be fairy, enemies of their kind."

"They put poison in the tunnels," murmured the thane. "They set traps in the kitchen."

Short Tail whispered, "They have the . . ." He stopped, then went on, "The tunnel—"

The other mice covered their ears. "Don't say!" they cried. "Don't say its name! Bad thing, bad thing!"

Small mice sobbed and clung to their mothers. "Don't let it come, Mama," one sobbed.

Kieryn looked as puzzled as I felt, but Brynn crept closer to his sister and touched her paw, as fearful as the other mice. "They means the tunnel beast," he whispered. "*Him* sends it in to kill them."

"What do ye mean?" Kieryn asked. "What be a tunnel beast?"

"Wicked sharp teeth, furry, size of small cat but stretched out long and thin. Fierce."

"A ferret," I whispered. "Is that what you mean?"

Brynn glanced at me. "Tunnel beast," he repeated. "Very bad. *Him* keeps in cage."

The mice watched us, atwitch with fear and worry. I heard several mutter it was our fault. We'd shown Ashbourne the tunnel's opening. He'd send the, the—he'd send the unspeakable thing in after them. They'd all die.

The thane nodded and turned to the others. "We must flee or face certain death. Take the escape routes now. Don't wait until we hear it coming."

The mice scattered at once, running this way and that into the dark labyrinth of tunnels branching off the meeting hall.

"Wait!" Kieryn called after them. "We don't know the way!"

No one answered, no one waited. And from above, we heard a new sound. Something was pushing and shoving its way into the tunnel, squeezing downward. We had no choice but to follow the scuffling, squeaking mouse sounds as best we could.

Closer and closer the tunnel beast came—the ferret, bred long and thin to wiggle into narrow places and kill mice and rats. Onward we fled into the darkness, our mouse hearts pounding. As a girl, I'd had no need to fear a ferret. Detestable as the creature was, the most it could do was bite me. I was much too big for it to kill me.

But as a mouse, I had plenty to fear from a ferret.

Kieryn stopped suddenly and turned to Brynn and me. "The tunnel beast be gaining on us. As mousies, we cannot escape it." She raised her paws as Brynn began squeaking in dismay. "Oh, don't be such a timmytim. Listen to me. We must change ourselves to small beasties. Ants, I reckon, be best."

By now we could hear the ferret growling as it burrowed after us. Its breath seemed to warm the air at my back. I smelled its stink.

Kieryn drew us close and began one of her chants. Brynn and I said it after her, all three of us trembling so hard we could barely speak. "Little, little, black and shiny, hide in the earth, ant, ant, ant. Fierce biter, soldier, little, little, little, dig in the dirt, ant, ant, ant."

Once more we shrank, squeezing ourselves painfully into

tiny, hard bodies. Just behind us, I glimpsed the ferret's face, mouth wide, sharp teeth shining. He snarled, clearly baffled by his prey's disappearance.

Like Kieryn and Brynn, I scurried down the tunnel as fast as an ant can go, climbing over clods of dirt and rubble. At last we tumbled out into what we guessed was the cellar. We lay still and listened for sounds from the tunnel. All was silent. If we were lucky, the ferret had given up.

Brynn and I looked at Kieryn, waiting for her to tell us to return to our normal shapes. She shook her narrow, pointed head and led us across the floor, close to the wall. It was hard work being an ant. The smallest distances seemed enormous. Finally, we came to a door. Its top stretched upward into darkness, but the crack at the bottom was more than tall enough for us to slip through—one advantage, I supposed, of being an ant.

Outside, the lawn lay before us, a dense, dark forest of towering grass. A brightness spread across it; whether from the moon or a porch light, I couldn't say. Such things were too far above my head to see.

Wearily, I followed Kieryn and Brynn into the grass, navigating my way over and around twigs and stones.

At last, Kieryn stopped and allowed us to rest. "This be stupid," Brynn said crossly. "Let's be us'n. I hates being an ant."

"Not us'n," Kieryn replied. "Not yet. We be in danger still."

"Mice, then," Brynn muttered. "I won't take one more step if I gots to be a dimbob ant."

Kieryn thought it over, her antennae twitching with concentration. "Squirrels," she said.

We huddled together and Kieryn led us once more in a chant. "Squirrels, squirrels, squirrels. Bushy tails, bright eyes, quick and clever. Runners, jumpers, climbers. Treetop nesters, acorn hiders, treetop travelers. Squirrels, squirrels, squirrels."

In another agonizing flash of pain, we burst out of our tiny ant bodies and exploded into squirrels. My heart beat quickly and blood surged through my body, warming me. I saw the moon, high in the sky, and the big house rearing up from the lawn. Light blazed from its windows. A door opened, framing Mr. Ashbourne and his servants. Simkins aimed a flashlight across the grass.

By the time the light reached the trees, we were hiding high in a dense oak, three gray squirrels like any others.

"Don't move," Kieryn whispered. "Squirrels be daylight creatures. They sleeps at night."

Frozen with fear, I watched Mr. Ashbourne take a cage from Rose. Slowly he opened its door. "Find them," he cried. "Whether they be things that crawl or creep or fly, *find them!*"

An owl stepped from the cage and spread its wings. For a second, it clung to Mr. Ashbourne's wrist, its head turned toward him as if it understood what he was saying. Then it lifted itself into the air and flew low across the grass, its wings soundless as it searched.

"Quick." Kieryn darted into a hole in the tree trunk, and Brynn and I crowded in after her. "For now we be safe from yon wicked one."

Minutes passed. Every now and then we heard Mr. Ashbourne call to the owl. The owl called back, his hooting cry terrifying in the dark silence. He was close, too close, drawing nearer and nearer.

Suddenly, he alit on the branch right outside our hole and searched our hiding place with eyes the color of amber glass. His head swiveled away, and he hooted softly. Once more we changed—beetles this time, small enough to hide deeper in the tree.

"Go after them, Simkins!" Ashbourne shouted.

"But, sir," Simkins whined, "I don't know how to climb a tree. I might fall, I might hurt myself."

"*I'll* hurt you if you don't do as I say!"

Simkins mumbled and muttered, but we heard him begin to climb. Every now and then he slipped and groaned in fear, but at last he reached our hiding place. The owl moved aside and the man peered into the hole, probing the darkness with a flashlight.

"Have you got them?" Ashbourne cried.

"I don't see 'em anywhere, sir," Simkins answered. "They must've changed to something else, the clever monkeys." Simkins began to climb down slowly. The owl hovered a moment and then flew after him.

"Not clever enough," Mr. Ashbourne said. "I've called Moura. She's coming with the hound. Stay here and watch the tree until she arrives."

I heard Simkins mutter something to himself about staying out in the damp with his arthritis; it was bound to be bad for him, he'd ache all day tomorrow. I noticed he didn't speak loudly enough for his master to hear.

"We'd best move on," Kieryn whispered. "The pishy fool can sit there all night, but he'll never see us up here. Or where we go."

Brynn and I followed her out of the hole to a branch. From there, we made our slow beetle way from leaf to leaf, inch by inch. Tired and hungry, I surprised myself by nibbling leaves as if I really were an insect.

"Stop," Kieryn said. "This be too slow. I say we go back to squirrel shape, up high, running and jumping, quick, quick, quick, out of the hound's reach."

In a second, we were running along branches that swayed under our weight, leaping from one tree to the next. The ground was far below, but as a squirrel, I had no fear of falling.

At one point, we came to a road and saw headlights. We hid among the leaves and watched Moura's sports car pass beneath us. Cadoc leaned out of a window, sniffing the air. Suddenly, he barked sharply, and the car stopped so fast it rocked.

"Be still," Kieryn whispered. "That fusty hound can't climb up here. Nor can *her,* old witchy witch that she be."

The car door opened and Moura stepped out, her face pale in the moonlight. Cadoc slid out beside her, long and lean and agile.

Moura looked up into the trees. "I know you're there," she said. "If you come down now, I will spare you."

Cadoc growled and bared his teeth. Maybe he'd spare us. Most likely, he wouldn't.

15

"COME DOWN, I SAY," Moura called. "I've had enough of your defiance."

But we were already gone—three bats winging our way through the night, heading for home, the wind in our faces, high above fields and woods. Flying. Flying.

At last, we came to rest on the tower's roof and perched there, surveying the scene. Lights blazed from the windows of the house, but all was silent inside. Deserted. Moura was gone, we knew that, but where was Dad?

"There he be." Kieryn fluttered a wing toward the woods. Dad stepped out of the trees, swinging a flashlight from side to side. "Jen," he called. "Jen!"

He was looking for me, searching the woods, frantic. "Jen!" he called again. "Jen, where are you?"

"Come." Kieryn led Brynn and me to a chimney on the roof of the house. Down we went, through the grime and soot, until we tumbled out on the dining room hearth.

We flew silently to my room and huddled on my bed, three bedraggled bats, black with soot.

"Be Jen again," Kieryn squeaked.

I'd gotten faster at transforming myself from one thing to another. By the time I heard Dad downstairs, I was myself, dressed, face washed, but still trying to think of an explanation for my disappearance—and reappearance.

Kieryn and Brynn dove under the bed with Tink, who seemed totally unperturbed to see two gray kittens instead of one. Like me, I supposed nothing could surprise him now.

I stepped into the hall and leaned over the railing. Dad was pacing up and down right beneath me.

"What's going on?" I called.

Dad jumped at the sound of my voice and stared at me in amazement. He ran up the stairs and grasped my shoulders. "I've looked *everywhere* for you. Moura's searching the roads right now. I was about to call the police."

"I'm sorry, Dad. I didn't mean to worry you, but I took a long walk in the woods," I lied. "When I came home, no one was here. I thought you'd gone somewhere without me. So I went up to my room, and I guess I fell asleep."

It was a feeble story but certainly more believable than the truth. Hoping to add credibility, I yawned and rubbed my eyes.

Dad hugged me. "You must have come in while Moura and I were outside looking for you. We never thought to check your room again."

He held me at arm's length, his face serious. "I should be angry with you," he said, "but all I feel right now is relief. Moura was sure something dreadful had happened to you."

I remembered Moura standing in the road, staring into the treetops. If she'd caught us, something dreadful *would* have happened to me. And to Kieryn and Brynn as well.

"But here you are," Dad went on, "safe and sound."

At that moment, a car pulled into the driveway and braked sharply to a stop. Dad and I went to the head of the stairs to see who it was, although I was pretty sure I knew. Seconds later, Moura opened the front door and stared up at me, shocked, I supposed, to see me standing there. Cadoc stood beside her, his eerie eyes on me, and growled.

Dad smiled at Moura. "Look who's here," he said. "It seems Jen came home while we were searching the woods for her and fell asleep in her room. Isn't that something?"

Moura forced a smile in return. "We were so worried about you, Jen."

While Dad watched happily, she ran up the steps and gave me a hug. "Such a naughty girl to frighten your father," she said with a laugh. In a lower voice, she added, "You and I will talk later, my dear."

I backed away, chilled to the bone. "There's nothing to talk about," I said as lightly as I could.

"It's very late," Dad said, "but let's go downstairs and sit for a while. I'm too keyed up to go to sleep."

We followed him to the living room. Moura sank down onto the sofa, and Cadoc settled himself at her feet, his eyes following me as I took a seat in the armchair opposite her.

"I'd love a cup of peppermint tea," I told Dad. "And something to eat—cheese and crackers maybe?"

"A glass of red wine for me," Moura said, "if you don't mind."

"Of course."

As soon as Dad left the room, she leaned toward me, giving me the full power of her witchy eyes. "What silly game are you playing? The creatures you're protecting are wicked. Dangerous. They were kept in those traps for a good reason."

Her perfume wafted toward me, fuzzing everything. Frightened, I pressed myself against the back of the chair. "It's not a silly game," I whispered. "I know what you are."

"You have no idea what I am—or what I can do." Moura leaned closer to me, dizzying me with her musky scent. "If you have any sense, you'll tell me where those creatures are."

"I'll never tell you. Never!" I tried to turn my head away, but her eyes held me.

She laughed softly. "You are indeed a foolish girl to trust those two. They'll betray you in the end, you know. It's their nature to lie and deceive."

"Speak for yourself," I whispered.

"Give Kieryn and Brynn to me," Moura said, "and I will leave. No harm to you, no harm to your father. Do you understand?"

Cadoc looked at me and growled softly. Moura rested her hand on the hound's head and waited for me to answer. In the kitchen, the tea kettle began to whistle.

I stared at her, scared of the hatred in her eyes. "I won't

give them to you." My voice sounded small and weak. "You can't make me."

She shrugged and flicked a dog hair from her skirt. "I'll get them one way or another, my dear Jen."

When Dad came in with a tray, Moura darted a quick look at me and whispered, "You'll regret this." Turning to Dad, she smiled and took a glass of blood red wine from him. "Lovely, Hugh, lovely!"

After handing me my tea and a plate of cheese and crackers, Dad sat down beside Moura and raised his wineglass. "Here's to Jen," he said. "May she always return safely from her adventures."

Moura murmured something and clinked her glass against his. Glancing at me, she raised an eyebrow as if to say I would not return safely from my next adventure.

I sat with them for a while, but Moura captured Dad's attention with questions about his opinions of various artists. She listened to his answers, nodding her head in agreement with his views. "Yes," she would murmur, "I have often thought the same—Pissarro has been underestimated, undervalued."

I was of no interest to anyone but Cadoc, who watched me with unblinking eyes. A corner of his mouth lifted in a silent snarl, as if he were waiting for an excuse to attack me.

While Dad refilled Moura's wineglass, I said good night and carried my cup and saucer to the kitchen. There I filled a bag with more cheese and crackers, as well as apples and raisins. In the living room, Moura and Dad went on talking.

Taking care not to be seen with a bag of food, I sneaked up to my room. Kieryn and Brynn purred and ran to meet me. After I locked the door, they changed from cats to girl and boy and sat down beside me, devouring the food I'd brought.

Kieryn wiped crumbs from her mouth and patted her tummy. She purred just like Tink, even though she was now a girl. "What did *her* tell ye down there?" she asked. "We heard *her* voice but not *her* skitzy words."

"She said you and Brynn are dangerous. She wants to save me from you."

"Oh, *her*'s a wicked one indeed, to play the old switcheroo game," Kieryn said. "Turn and twist, twist and turn, that's *her* way and no mistake."

Solemn-faced, Brynn slid closer to his big sister. "But what if *her* tricks Jen? Ye know how witches be with their spells and lies." He shot me a distrustful look. "Jen don't know *her* the way we do."

"Don't ye worry." Kieryn hugged Brynn. "*Her* can't fool our Jen. She be a clever girl. And getting braver every day."

But Brynn continued to look at me with suspicion. "She be human," he muttered to his sister. "There be bad suss between our kinkind and hers. I say, Don't trust no one but me."

Kieryn ignored her brother. Turning her odd tilted eyes to me, she asked, "What else did *her* tell ye?"

"She said if I give you and Brynn to her, she'll leave without harming Dad or me."

"And if ye don't?" Kieryn asked.

"She didn't actually say what she'd do." My voice shook a little. "She wouldn't harm Dad, would she?"

Kieryn shuddered. "There be no telling what *her* might do."

Brynn took his sister's hand and pulled her away from me. "We be fairykind. We don't need no human mucking about with us. She'll just make trouble."

I grabbed Kieryn's other hand. "There must be a way to get rid of Moura."

Kieryn's eyes lit with green fire. "Why, 'tis clear enough, ain't it? We must trap *him* and *her* like they done us."

"But I broke all the traps," I said.

"Nae," Kieryn said. "There be more. Yer kind been using them since old times back and back and long agone. Does *her* not have a shop?"

"Yes, the Dark Side of the Moon." I stared at Kieryn, perplexed. "But why would she have something so dangerous to herself?"

"I already told ye, they got them glasses," Kieryn said impatiently. "Don't ye remember? They protect their skitzy eyes."

"That's why *his* attic was chock-full of traps," Brynn put in. "They gets all they can and hides 'em away so they won't come upon one, unexpected-like."

"So all we need do is go to *her* shop and find two traps. Then we steal their glasses, and quick as quick into the globes they go," Kieryn cried. "Trapped!"

Brynn bounced up and down on the bed, his spiky hair flying around his face. "Then *bam!* go the stoppers into the spouts, snickety-snick. No more *her* or *him!* They be in there forever and always."

"Jen?" Dad's voice shattered our excitement. He was outside the door, his hand on the knob. "Why is the door locked?"

In a second, Kieryn and Brynn changed themselves to kittens and darted under the bed with Tink.

I opened the door. Dad and Moura stood together in the hall.

"Who were you talking to?" Dad asked.

"Nobody."

"But we heard you," Moura said softly.

"It sounded as if you had company." Dad looked around the room as if he expected to see someone.

"Oh, I was talking to Tink and Mist. Telling them a story. With voices—like you used to do when you read to me. Remember?" I was talking too fast, saying too much, but I couldn't stop myself.

Tink came out from under the bed and rubbed against Dad's legs. In the dark hall, Cadoc growled and slunk toward the cat. Moura laid her hand on his head and murmured something. The dog whined and sat down beside her.

"Where is Mist?" Moura asked.

Before I could answer, she was down on her knees beside the bed. In a moment, she sprang back up, a squirming kitten in each hand. Tink hissed at her, but she wasn't interested in him, only in the two she'd captured.

"Look," she said to Dad, "Jen's brought home another stray."

"Give them to me." I reached for the kittens, but Moura stepped away. "They're mine."

"Jen," Dad said. "Where did the second one come from?"

"The woods," I stammered, "just like Mist. Make her give them to me, Dad."

"Feral cats don't make good pets," Moura said. "Just look at the way they're snarling at me. They'd love to scratch my eyes out."

Forgetting everything but Kieryn and Brynn, I flung myself at Moura and grabbed at the kittens. "Give them to me, you witch!"

"Jen!" Dad seized me and pulled me away from Moura. "What are you doing? Control yourself!"

Moura strode toward the door, holding the kittens by the nape of their necks. They struggled, their fur bristled, their tails lashed, they yowled and hissed. "You can't allow Jen to behave like this," Moura told Dad. "She must be punished."

I fought Dad, pummeling him with my fists, kicking at his legs, flailing this way and that. "Let me go!" I screamed. "Don't let that witch take my kittens! She'll hurt them."

Moura went out into the hall, followed by Cadoc. He rose up on his hind legs and snapped at Brynn and Kieryn. "Not yet," Moura whispered to the dog. "Be patient."

Dad looked at me in despair. "Jen, what's happened to change you so? How can you be so hateful?"

I clung to him and begged him not to listen to Moura, but he pushed me away and left the room. The door slammed shut.

"Lock it," I heard Moura say. "She won't stay there unless you do."

"But—" Dad began.

"You must punish her," Moura cut in. "She was rude to me. Disrespectful. I cannot possibly marry you if you allow your daughter to say and do whatever she pleases."

"But, Moura," Dad began again.

"She's a liar as well." Moura went on as if Dad hadn't spoken. "I don't believe she was sleeping up here while we searched for her. Heaven knows where she was or what she was doing. She'll be completely out of control if you don't put an end to this right now."

"Jen never used to act like this." Dad's voice broke. "I don't know what's wrong with her."

I'd heard enough. I ran to the door and pounded on it. "Dad," I cried. "Dad, can't you see what's she doing? It's her fault things have changed. She's evil, she's—"

"Put a stop to it," Moura hissed at Dad. "Or I swear I will walk out of this house and never return."

“That’s enough, Jen,” Dad said, his voice suddenly cold and firm. “Stay here and think about your behavior.”

The key turned in the lock.

The kittens cried once in distress. Moura’s quick, sharp steps clattered down the stairs. Cadoc’s toenails clicked behind her. Dad followed more slowly.

I lay on the floor and looked under my door at the empty hall. Maybe Kieryn and Brynn would come scampering back on mouse feet or hopping on cricket legs or slithering on snake bellies. Surely they’d find a way to escape from Moura.

I waited. And waited. And waited. The wooden floor grew harder. And colder.

But nothing came—not a mouse, not a cricket, not a snake. Kieryn and Brynn weren’t strong enough to escape from Moura. Unless I could figure out a way to rescue them, she would trap them again—forever this time.

16

HOURS LATER, LONG before dawn, I woke up, stiff from sleeping on the floor. Moonlight filled my room. My walls were patterned with swaying shadows cast by the trees outside. The house was dead silent.

I stood up and tried the door. Still locked. I pounded on it anyway, hoping Dad would hear me and relent. But even though I beat on the wood till my fists ached, no one came.

Tink meowed from the windowsill. I ran to his side and poked my head out into the cool night air. The lawn lay far below, silver where the moonlight struck it. Dad's new shovel lay beside the flower bed, its newly turned earth a dark patch in the grass. He must have started working on it after Mr. Ashbourne left with the paintings.

If Kieryn had been with me, I could have become a bat or a bird and flown out of my room. But without her help, I couldn't change my shape. No matter how hard I concentrated on wings and tails and feathers, I remained a girl.

"Oh, Tink," I whispered. "How can I save Kieryn and Brynn?"

His tail swished back and forth. He hunched forward and

stretched his neck to peer at the shadowy lawn. In the darkness under the oak tree, something moved. Tink and I drew back, afraid it was Moura.

Below my window, a strange old woman stepped cautiously into the moonlight. Her back was bent, and she leaned heavily on a cane, but she wore big black hiking boots with yellow shoelaces, purple- and pink-striped stockings, a yellow polka-dot dress with lace trim, and an enormous black straw hat strewn with flowers. To top it off, her long, bushy hair was Day-Glo pink. Shading her eyes with one hand, she surveyed the house. After a moment, she beckoned, and two more old women joined her.

The first was tall and skinny, and the second was short and fat. The tall one wore a long, loose purple dress that floated around her like gauze. Her hat was lime green and hugged her head like a cloche, hiding all her features except a pointed nose and chin. The hair spilling down her back was a glorious blue. On her feet she wore ankle-high red tennis shoes with spike heels.

The short one's wild mop of curly green hair burst from under a tiny red and yellow beanie. Her tent-shaped dress was covered with flowers in bright colors, and her shoes were orange with platform soles.

I blinked twice, three times, and rubbed my eyes, sure I was dreaming. But even after I'd pinched myself, the trio refused to vanish.

"Where do ye think *her* be?" the leader asked.

"In yon big housie," the short one said.

"It's a big, big, bigsy housie," the tall one observed in a mournful voice. "We'll never find *her,* search as we will."

"Nae fear," the short one said. "We'll sniff *her* out like we always does. *Her* canna hide from us."

Dropping to her knees, the leader began to crawl toward the house, sniffing the grass like a dog on the track of something.

The others joined her, circling and sniffing. Gradually, both Tink and I relaxed. The old women didn't seem dangerous—just very, very odd.

Suddenly, I remembered the flashes of light I'd seen when I broke the glass globes in Mr. Ashbourne's tower. Turning to the cat, I whispered, "It's the aunties, Tink! They must be looking for Moura."

Tink leaned out the window and meowed loudly. I grabbed him, afraid he'd fall, and the old women looked up at me in surprise.

"It be the human child," the leader cried. "Her who saved us!"

Leaping to their feet, all three curtsied and bobbed around, bowing their heads.

"Thank'ee, thank'ee!" they called. "Thank'ee ten times over the moon, a hundred times over the sun, and a dozen times in and out of the rainbow for breaking them cursed jimjams, them geegaws, them wicked trapsters. Thank'ee, thank'ee, thank'ee, young miss."

"You're the aunties," I said. "You were in the traps I broke."

"Oh, aye, we be the aunties," the leader said. "And fairies, too."

"We be yer good fairies," the tall one said. "Nice to those that be nice to us. Not to be feared or spoke ill of. But to those that do us wicked, we—"

"In short, for Skilda do go on and on," the leader interrupted, "we share no kinkind with *her* that hides in yer housie."

"Can ye show us the way to *her* lair?" the short one asked.

"I'm locked in my room," I told them. "She made my father punish me. She took Kieryn and Brynn."

The aunties drew close together and stared at me in dismay. "Nae, it can't be," the leader whispered. "Them two be too young to fight *her.* They be helpless as real kittens in her hands."

Skilda began to weep. "*Her* will destroy them."

The short one cried. "Withouten the childern, there be no way home for us."

The leader hugged both. "Gugi, dinna cry and fash yerself. Skilda, cease yer tiresome tears. We ain't defeated as easy as *her* believes. We'll save our wee kinkind, never doubt it."

"Oh, Binna," Skilda sobbed. "*Her* be too strong—many and many times too strong."

"And *him* will come to help," Gugi added. "*He*'ll bring more traps."

"Shut yer gaping big mouths," Binna said. "And listen to

me. Both of ye. The human girl up there will take us to *her.* We'll sort things out right smart."

Gugi and Skilda did their best to be quiet, but their faces were full of misery and fear. I doubted Skilda could look happy even if she tried, but Gugi seemed made for laughing, not weeping.

"But she be locked in," Gugi reminded Binna.

Binna looked up at me. "Ye must jump."

"Jump?" I stared down, way down, at the three aunties. "I'd break both legs when I hit the ground. Maybe even die."

"Ye won't be hurt, timmytim," Binna said. "We have magic, ye know."

"But—"

"Just do it," Binna said. "Too much thinking do more harm than good, don't ye know?"

The three of them moved even closer together and formed a triangle below my window. They spread their arms. "Close yer eyes and jump. We'll catch ye with our magic, no harm."

I glanced at Tink. Before I realized what he was doing, he'd leapt out the window. I leaned out after him. "My cat!"

The aunties caught him.

"There, ye see how quick and easy it's done?" cried Gugi.

"Tink says he'd do it again if he could," Binna told me. "It were great fun—like a birdie flying through the air."

Safe in Skilda's arms, Tink peered up at me. If he could do it, so could I. Slowly I stepped onto the windowsill. Far below, Skilda set Tink down, and the three aunties spread their arms to catch me as they'd caught my cat.

Behind me was my room and my cozy bed. In front of me was the sky. Just beyond the treetops, the tower rose dark against the stars. A dim light glowed in its windows. Could Moura be there with Kieryn and Brynn?

I looked down. The three aunties looked up. So did Tink. He had nine lives. I had one. If those good fairies failed me, if they dropped me, if I fell—well, as Binna said, thinking did more harm than good. Moura had to be stopped.

I spread my arms. The night air kissed my face with cold. Taking a deep breath, I jumped.

17

TINK WAS RIGHT. It was glorious, just like flying. With barely a jolt, I landed in the aunties' arms. *Bounce, bounce*—and there I was, beside them. The dew on the grass chilled my bare feet.

"Aha!" cried Gugi. "That were as easy as snog whistling!"

I had no idea what snog whistling was, but I nodded enthusiastically. It hadn't just been easy, it had been fun—the same feeling you have when you finally jump off the high dive, splash into the water like a fish, and can't wait to do it again.

"Now, show us where *her* be," Binna said. "For I fear we have no time to waste."

I pointed to the small lighted windows under the eaves of the tower. "I think she's up there."

The aunties studied the windows silently. After a few moments, Binna turned to me. "Did Kieryn share with ye the ways of changing shape?"

"Yes, but I can't do it by myself. I tried before you got here. But it just didn't work."

"We be of the belief that bats be the best choice," Binna

went on. "We can help ye be a bat with us, but if ye dinna care to change, ye can wait here."

"I know all about being a bat," I told them, eager to fly again.

The aunties took my hands and we formed a circle on the grass. They mumbled and swayed and talked in odd rhymes in a language I didn't know. I felt familiar sharp pains shoot through me, and in a moment all four of us were circling upward. Left behind, Tink mewed.

Slowly we flew around the tower, peering in each window we passed. Moura was standing in the center of the room. In each hand she held a kitten by the nape of its neck. Kieryn and Brynn twisted and thrashed and yowled, but they couldn't free themselves. Moura regarded them, her eyes hidden by those glasses. At her feet, Cadoc watched, snapping at the kittens whenever he thought they might be in reach of his long, cruel muzzle.

The aunties settled themselves in the ivy by an open window, and I snuggled beside them, loving the feel of my wings wrapped around me.

"What do we do now?" Skilda whispered.

Binna frowned. "Patience, ye great twit. I be thinking on it."

"Me, too," Gugi said. "But I ain't be coming up with answers."

In the tower, Moura spoke. "You can struggle all you wish, fairy spawn, but you won't escape this time. Ciril is on his way with traps so powerful that no human can break them, either accidentally or deliberately."

The kittens hissed and growled. Moura laughed. Cadoc rose on his hind legs and snapped. Moura raised the kittens higher. "They are not for you, hound!"

"Why can't they change shapes?" I whispered to Binna. "That's what we did before."

Binna sighed. "They be too young—fledglings, like. Their magic's not yet strong enough to defy *her*."

"That's what I thought." I peered in the window again. Moura was holding Kieryn upside down by her tail, encouraging Cadoc to snap at her. I turned away, unable to watch.

"Surely you can do something," I said to Binna.

"Let me mull a wee while longer." Binna flipped upside down and hid her face in her wings. Gugi and Skilda did the same. And so did I. There we hung, four bats in a row, rocked gently by the wind in the ivy.

At last Binna unfolded her wings and peered down at the moonlit lawn. "*Him* approaches," she squeaked.

No sooner had she spoken than Ashbourne stepped cautiously out of the trees. He paused on the edge of the shadows, a slim figure dressed in black, his eyes shielded by glasses. Behind him Simkins clutched two dark bags, waiting faithfully for his master to speak.

Ashbourne was in no hurry. First he surveyed the lawn, then the house. No lights, no motion, no sound. Dad slept soundly, oblivious to everything. I knew nothing short of an explosion would wake him. Once he fell asleep, he was gone.

The only one watching was Tink. He sat on the terrace, as still as a statue of an Egyptian cat. No one noticed him but me.

Ashbourne turned his attention to the tower. All four of us snuggled deeper into the ivy, fearful he might see through our disguise.

At last, he left the safety of the shadows and glided across the grass, his shadow skimming along beside him. Simkins followed closely. I heard something in the bags clink.

"The traps," Binna hissed. Skilda moaned and Gugi squeaked.

At the foot of the tower, the two stopped again and looked toward the house. Still no lights, no motion, no sound. Dad slept on, undisturbed.

We heard the door screech as it opened. Moura called, "Is that you, Ciril?"

"Who else?" Ashbourne climbed the steps, his feet heavy on the treads.

"Have you brought the traps?"

"Of course."

Binna beckoned me to take her place at the window. "Be my eyes," she whispered. "I dare not look for fear them traps will draw me in once more."

I peeked out of the ivy. Through my bat eyes, the room was dim, blurry, out of focus, but I could see well enough to make out Moura, Ashbourne, and Simkins, as well as the two frightened kittens. With a flourish, Ashbourne took the bags from Simkins and pulled out the globes. They were magnificent, swirling with patterns of deep crimson, gold, and indigo.

Kieryn and Brynn closed their eyes and yowled, they twisted and flailed, they raked at Moura with their claws. Cursing, she urged Ashbourne to thrust the traps so close that the globes bounced against their bodies. Even though they couldn't see the colors, they must have felt their pull. With one last desperate meow, Brynn vanished. Though she fought for another moment or two, Kieryn disappeared into the other trap, sucked through the little spout in a flash.

Ashbourne pressed the stoppers into the spouts and laughed. "Now, my little friends," he cried, "let's see you escape this time!"

Beside me, the aunties burrowed deep into the ivy and wept tiny bat squeaks of despair. "Gone," Skilda sobbed. "Gone."

The two globes glowed with a fierce green light. They buzzed and vibrated, but Ashbourne thrust them back into the bags and handed them to Simkins.

"Hold on tight," he said. "Don't drop them."

"I'll be careful, sir. Indeed I will. You can trust old Simkins. The imps are safe in my hands." Simkins bowed and nodded and practically groveled at Ashbourne's feet.

What a wretch he was. I detested him with every cell of my body—bat and human both.

As if she read my thoughts, Binna whispered, "Do nae waste yerself hating him. Save yer strength for what's to come."

Swiftly, silently, we flew down from the window and watched the three emerge from the tower. With Cadoc loping ahead, they crossed the lawn, their shadows inky dark. Tink still sat on the terrace, unmoving, cloaked in darkness. If the hound saw him, he gave no sign. I supposed bigger things were afoot.

As they entered the woods, Simkins plucked at Ashbourne's sleeve. "Please don't forget your promise, sir."

Ashbourne turned to his servant. "Promise? What promise?"

"A few drops of their blood, sir, that's what you promised me. Just a little. You must remember, sir."

I turned to the aunties in horror. "Their blood? Ashbourne promised Simkins some of Kieryn's and Brynn's blood?"

They chittered to one another in bat-speak, too low and too fast for me to understand. "Tell me what you're saying," I begged.

"Oh, there be a legend that says drink a drop or two of fairy blood and live forever and always." Binna stretched her wings and grinned. "But most legends don't tell the whole truth of it, as yon Simkins may learn."

"Beware, be wary ware what ye ask for when ye deal wi' fairies and witches," Gugi added.

"Nae, don't ye be scaring wee Jen, ye great bogey," Skilda put in. "She need na fear us."

"Nor should she trust us," said Gugi in a voice so low I wasn't certain I'd heard her right. Surely I could trust the aunties. If they meant to harm me, they would have done so before now. Instead, they'd done their best to keep me safe.

From below, Moura cried, "Tell me you made no such promise, Ciril!"

Startled by the anger in her voice, Cadoc growled at Ashbourne. The man took a step back and bumped into Simkins, who began yammering apologies for being in the way.

Ignoring his servant's humble pleas, Ashbourne said, "I must speak to Moura in private. I have not apprised her of our agreement."

Simkins clutched the bags to his chest, causing an outburst of buzzing sounds and flashing light. "Please, sir, I've done much for you. Taken risks, endangered my pitiful mortal self. Not that I complain, sir. I live to serve—"

"Never fear," Ashbourne interrupted. "Simply trust me, my good servant. Indeed, I owe much to you."

If I'd been Simkins, I wouldn't have believed a word Ashbourne said, but the man nodded and bowed and watched his master lead Moura deeper into the trees. We four flew silently after them and hid ourselves in the branches over their heads.

"You must be mad," Moura whispered. "You cannot give a mortal man fairy blood, not even a drop. Do you want that baseborn clown to become as we are?"

"Hush." Ashbourne covered her mouth with his hand. "And hear me out."

I, for one, was glad Moura was still wearing her glasses. I didn't want to see the look in her eyes. She said nothing, and he continued, keeping his voice so low that I was grateful for my sharp bat ears.

"I promised him the blood in order to gain his help and cooperation," Ashbourne went on. "He has done more for our cause than you will ever know. Mortals can be useful guides in this sad world."

"But—"

"I said, Hush." Ashbourne spoke with anger, and Moura drew back. Cadoc growled but stayed beside his mistress.

"What is promised is not always given," Ashbourne went on. "In this case, will *not* be given. When we are ready to return to our world, I shall dispose of him."

"Ah." Moura let out her breath in a satisfied sigh. "I apologize, Ciril. I should have known."

Without acknowledging her apology, Ashbourne spun on his heel and strode back to Simkins. "All's well, my man. I have Moura's approval."

Simkins shot Moura a small smile, more of a leer. "Thank you, miss. It's good of you. Very good. I won't forget your kindness, your generosity, your—"

"Enough." Moura strode off into the woods ahead of the others, and we followed, invisible in the treetops.

"Where are we taking them, sir?" Simkins asked, still struggling with the twitching bags.

"Not to my house," Ashbourne said. "That hateful child may find her way back there."

"I think not," Moura muttered. "I've convinced her father to place her under my supervision. I've planned a shopping trip tomorrow." She paused and smiled. "I have a strange presentiment the child may come to harm somehow. An accident perhaps. Maybe a kidnapping. A disappearance. . . . All quite mysterious."

The sound of their laughter both angered and scared me. Chilled, I moved closer to Binna, eager to feel her warmth. A shopping trip, a disappearance—we'd see about that. If I'd had the courage, I would have swooped into Moura's hair and bitten her neck.

"But, sir," Simkins whined, "you haven't told me where we're taking the fairy spawn."

"It's not necessary for you to know everything," Moura snapped.

By this time, the three had reached the road where the car waited, silvery and sleek in the moonlight. Unlocking the doors, Ashbourne ushered Moura into the front seat and Simkins into the back, along with his bags. As silently as a cat, Cadoc leapt in beside Moura. Ashbourne slid behind the wheel and closed the door. The engine started quickly, almost silently, and the car raced away toward town.

Unknown to the driver or his passengers, four bats flew after it, barely stirring the air with our wings. I hoped Kieryn knew we were near.

18

JUST AS I'D EXPECTED, Ashbourne stopped outside the antique store. All the houses and shops were dark, their doors shut and locked against the night. Even the streetlights were out. Silently we watched Moura lead the others inside, Cadoc first and Simkins last, as usual. With a muffled thump, the door closed behind them. Nothing stirred but the leaves.

"Now what?" I asked the aunties.

Binna, Skilda, and Gugi looked at one another. After a brief pause, Binna said, "First we rescues the wee ones. Then, then—well, I reckon we'll think of something."

"Kieryn had an idea," I said softly, unsure whether I should suggest anything to the aunties. They obviously knew far more than I did about this sort of thing.

Binna turned to me hopefully. "And what were Kieryn's idea?"

"Well, she thought we should trap them the way they trapped all of you."

Gugi clapped her hands. "Yes, yes!" she cried. "In they go, and we hides 'em away, away, away."

"Long, long away," Skilda added. "Never to be seen anywhere, anytime, anywhen. *Poof!*"

"Hush now," Binna said. "First the rescue, then the punishment."

The aunties drew me into their circle and began their odd chitter-chatter. Another flash of pain, and my wings were gone, and so were theirs. On little pink mouse feet we crept up the sidewalk and squirmed under the door. Inside, the shop was dark and silent.

"Too bad mousies canna hear as well as bats," Skilda complained.

"But they sees better," Gugi said.

We scampered through the shop and headed for the rooms behind it. A slit of light shone under a closed door. We forced our small bodies into what seemed to be Moura's living room, filled with moonlight and shadows and dark furniture. Voices came from a room beyond.

"Stay close to the wall," Binna told us. "Make no sound. Move slow . . . oh, so slow . . . slower than slow."

"And beware the hound," Skilda added.

"For a dog may be worse than a cat," Gugi agreed.

In the next room, our three enemies huddled around the kitchen table, Moura shoulder to shoulder with Ashbourne, Simkins sitting apart, Cadoc restlessly pacing, toenails clicking against the tile floor. On the table were the balls, flashing with a duller light now, buzzing more quietly than the cicadas outside in the night.

Without looking at the traps, the aunties scurried under a cabinet and turned their pointed snouts to the wall.

"Watch them for us," Binna whispered to me. "We have no glasses to protect us."

Obediently, I crawled to the edge of the cabinet and peered up at Moura and her companions. Cadoc lay at his mistress's feet now, his muzzle resting on her shoes. My mouse heart beat so fast, I feared he'd hear it. Despite the hound's relaxed pose, I sensed it would take little to rouse him.

Moura tapped one of the globes with her long red nails and smiled. "First your silly aunties tried to keep you safe. Then Mostyn did his best. Like the aunties, the blundering old man failed. And so did that foolish girl. No one can defeat me, Kieryn. While you rot in this lovely prison, Ciril and I shall rule your land and enslave your kin."

"We still need the pendant," Ciril reminded Moura. "We can't go home without it."

Moura studied the globe. "You gave it to the human brat, didn't you, Kieryn?" She flashed Ashbourne a wicked smile. "No doubt you hid it in Jen's room, using silly childish spells. Don't worry. I'll find it after poor Jen's 'tragic accident.'"

The globe buzzed and flashed both green and purple, but Moura pushed it aside and turned to Ashbourne. "Would that we could kill them," she said. "And be rid of them once and for all."

Ashbourne sighed. "Unfortunately, their mother's spell of protection is too strong for us to break."

"But not strong enough to save them from our traps." Moura frowned at the globes. "That buzzing and flashing is very tiresome. Shall I remove them from our sight and hearing?"

"Please," Ashbourne said wearily. "Put them where they won't be found."

Moura returned the traps to the bags. As she rose from the table, Simkins gave her a worried look. "What about my reward, miss?"

She frowned. "Don't be so impatient. You'll receive what you demand before Ciril and I leave." She glanced at Ashbourne and smiled. "You have my word, Simkins."

"The fool," Binna whispered. "*Her* will give him something all right, but it won't be what the dummy dolt expects."

From my hiding place, I watched Moura stride to the cellar door and open it. Sticking close to the wall, I dashed after her and followed her down the steps. *Pitty-pat, pitty-pat, pitty-pat.* It was like jumping over a series of cliffs.

At the bottom, Moura went to the darkest corner and opened an ancient wooden chest. She laid the balls inside, closed the lid, and locked it with a tiny gold key. Moving her hands as if she were carving shapes in the air, she hummed an eerie tune that made my whiskers quiver.

"There, my little friends," she whispered. "See how you like *my* magic."

Brushing a cobweb from her black velvet skirt, Moura crossed the basement to the stairs. The climb back up was far harder than the climb down. By the time I reached the top, Moura had shut the cellar door. Luckily, the gap at the bottom was just big enough for a mouse to squeeze through.

The kitchen was deserted, but I heard voices in the hall. The three aunties came out from under the cabinet, twitching their noses.

"Where be the children?" Binna asked.

"In a trunk. Moura locked it and then cast a spell. A strong one, I think."

"Ah, don't ye worry, Jen," Gugi whispered, patting me with one little paw. "We'll figure a way of busting it. *Her* ain't the only one who knows magic."

"Come," Binna beckoned. "They be about to leave." We stole through the shop and crouched in the shadows of a tall chest of drawers.

Our enemies stood together at the open door. "I'll take care of the girl tomorrow," Moura was saying.

"And her father?" Ciril asked softly. "What of him?"

Moura's laugh tinkled like icicles breaking. "The poor fool loves me. He'll do what I say, believe what I tell him. He's of no consequence whatsoever."

I'd known all along that Moura cared nothing for my father, but to hear her say it filled me with anger. Poor Dad—if only he'd listened to me.

"What about the aunts?" Ashbourne asked.

"What about them?"

"They escaped when the girl broke the traps. Doesn't it worry you that they're free?"

Moura laughed. "Don't be ridiculous, Ciril. Those ancient

fairies don't know magic from toadstools. Let them stay here in this world. They'll fade into shadows soon enough."

"I suppose you're right, my dear. Yet—" Ashbourne frowned. "I'd feel better if they were bottled up in traps, too."

Moura kissed him lightly. "Trust me. Skilda, Binna, and Gugi are not a threat."

After Ashbourne and Simkins drove away, Moura lifted her arms as if to embrace the moon. Turning slowly in circles, she swayed to music only she could hear. Cadoc rose on his hind legs and joined the dance.

The night wind lifted her hair, and her skirt swirled. "Come, Cadoc!" she cried. "It's time to run."

We watched as the two of them raced down the street and vanished into the darkness, the hound several yards ahead of his mistress.

"*Her* be a creature of the night," Binna said, "sister of owls and wolves, daughter of the moon, as fearsome as yer worstest dream."

"Where has she gone?" I asked.

"Why, *her*'s running back to yer house," Skilda said. "Fast as the wind *her* is."

"And twice times ten as cold," Gugi added.

"Be bats again," cried Binna. "And follow them!"

This time my wings sprouted at once, and I found myself in the air, flying with the aunties. "Kieryn and Brynn!" I cried. "We can't leave them in the cellar."

"For now we must," Binna told me. "*Her* has plans, and we must make sure *her* fails."

"Do na' fash yerself," Gugi told me. "We'll save the wee ones. For now they be safe."

On we flew, faster, I was sure, than any normal bat. Down below on the moonlit road, we saw Moura and Cadoc running, faster, I knew, than any human or dog.

When the house came into view, I saw no lights in the windows, heard no sound but the wind stirring and tapping and murmuring. Inside, Dad slept. Ignorant. Trusting.

Soundlessly, Moura and Cadoc slipped through the front door, but the aunties and I flew to my bedroom window. Once inside, the aunties shrugged out of their bat shapes as easily as if they were changing clothes, and gathered around me, three of the strangest old women I'd ever seen.

With a wave of her hand and a few muttered words, Binna changed me back to myself. It happened so fast this time, I barely felt the pain.

My arms and shoulders ached from flying, and I was ready to sleep for a hundred years, but the aunties were too excited to let me rest.

Binna seized my hands and peered into my eyes. This close, I could see the rings of color in her irises, shading from green at the outside to purple near the pupils. They had almost the same hypnotic effect as Mr. Ashbourne's glasses. "Ye must go with *her* tomorrow, Jen," she said. "Ye must act as if ye know nothing about *her* plans for ye."

I cowered in her grip. "How can you say such a thing? You heard what she said. She means to get rid of me, to kill me. Don't you care—"

"Oh, quit your whinging," Binna cut in, her voice suddenly fierce. "We ain't the sort to desert a child. *Her* can't harm ye with us around!"

"Ye'll be safe as a tiny chick in its nest," Gugi put in, with a sweet smile. "That snarky witch ain't near as smart as *her* thinks *her* is."

"*Her*'s not got all the biggity big power," Skilda added. "We got strong magic of our own, child."

Binna patted my hand. "We'll be near, dear Jen, just out of sight—maybe flying, maybe creeping."

"Maybe crawling, maybe hopping. Maybe wiggling through the grass like vipers," Skilda put in, her voice dreamy. "Full of poison for *her* that's hurt us and ours."

I looked at all three aunties. They hadn't done such a great job of protecting Kieryn and Brynn. I said, "But—"

Binna didn't let me say another word. "Here's what ye must do, Jen," she said in a firm voice. "Ye must get *her* glasses and give them to me." She released my hands and sat back. "That's all we ask of ye."

Gugi smiled and stroked my hair. "Just that one small thing. *Her* spectacles, them with the colored lenses."

"A raindrop falling into the sea." Skilda kissed my cheek with lips as soft and dry as old rose petals. "That's how easy it be."

"And how do I get Moura's glasses?" I asked. "Just say 'Please'?"

"Ye'll think of something, for ye're a clever lass," Binna said with more confidence than I had.

"Oh, and one more thing," she added. "Bring the pendant with ye, for we can't go nowhere without it."

I stared at Binna. "But how will I stop Moura from taking it from me? With all her power, surely—"

She patted my arm and smiled. "Never fear, Jen. Our queen did her best magic on that stone. *Her* cannot get it unless ye give it to *her*. It be as simple as that."

"Well, she won't get it, then," I said. "I'd never give it to her!"

"Be wary," Binna warned. "Witches be tricksier than tricksy."

Turning to her companions, she snapped her fingers, and all three vanished. Just like that. *Snap*—and they were gone.

I looked under my bed, I peered into the trees outside, I studied the shadows on the lawn. I saw nothing but Tink stalking through a patch of moonlight. Whatever shape the aunties had taken was their secret. And so were their whereabouts.

Uneasily, I undressed and got into bed, far too worried to sleep. I didn't want to leave the house with Moura in the morning. Suppose what I'd heard Gugi whisper was true? Suppose I couldn't trust the aunties? Suppose they weren't strong enough to protect me?

But I had to save Kieryn and Brynn. Which meant there was nothing to do but go with Moura and hope the aunties kept their word.

19

ALTHOUGH I WAS SURE I hadn't slept a minute, the sun woke me a little before seven. The house was silent. No sound of Dad stumping around busying himself with home-improvement projects. No bacon-and-egg fragrance to tempt me out of bed. No coffee to tickle my nose with its morning smell.

Moving quietly, I pulled on a T-shirt and a pair of cargo shorts with deep pockets. Then I crawled under my bed and retrieved the jewelry box. I touched it fearfully, expecting a shock, but nothing happened. Either Kieryn's spell had failed or it had been directed at Moura and nobody else. I opened the lid, pulled the pendant from its hiding place, and slipped it into a small drawstring pouch. Tying the string tightly, I stuffed it into my pocket and snapped the flap, securing the pouch and its contents.

"Please help me keep it safe," I whispered in case the aunties were hovering nearby. A fly on the wall, a beetle on the ivy, a bird on the windowsill—they could be anywhere.

At the door, I hesitated, worried I was still locked in. The knob turned easily. While I'd slept, someone had unlocked it. Ignoring a twinge of fear, I stepped out into the empty hall. Sunlight slanted across the walls, stippling them with shadows from the leaves. Except for the silence, it seemed an ordinary morning.

Tink uncurled from his post at the top of the stairs and ran to meet me. I picked him up and cuddled him close. He purred and licked my nose as if I were a wayward kitten.

"Where's Dad?" I whispered.

If Tink knew, he wasn't telling.

"How about *her?* Where's the beautiful Miss Moura?"

Tink tensed and lashed his tail as if he knew exactly who I meant.

A hand touched my shoulder, and I whirled to face Moura. She'd come up behind me as silently as a cat herself. Tink squirmed and jumped out of my arms.

"I'm right here, Jen," she said softly.

"Where's Dad?"

"Still sleeping, I suppose." She smiled and took my arm as if nothing had happened between us. "How about breakfast?"

Loathing her touch, I pulled my arm free and followed her downstairs. Tink waited at the bottom, his slim body tense, his ears erect.

Moura opened the refrigerator door. "What are you in the mood for?"

"Just cereal." I went to the cupboard and reached for a bowl. "I can fix it myself."

"I could make you an omelet," she offered. "Cheese, tomatoes, fresh herbs."

I shook my head, suspicious of the herbs she might have in mind.

"Have it your way," she said. "While you can."

I looked up from the milk I was pouring on my raisin bran. "What do you mean?"

She smiled and busied herself making coffee. "You must realize you can no longer count on getting your way. Rudeness and disrespect will be punished, as they were last night. I'm simply giving you the opportunity to make a fresh start today." She shrugged and filled the coffee maker with water.

"Your father and I have reached an agreement," she continued. "He realizes he has spoiled you since your mother's death, given in to your every wish and whim. No longer."

Moura looked at me with open dislike. "He has no problem with my disciplining you. Indeed, he thinks I'll do a better job than he has."

Dad chose that moment to appear in the doorway behind Moura. His smile disappeared when he saw the expression on my face. "Jen, surely you're not quarreling with Moura again. What's gotten into you?"

"Me? Nothing's gotten into *me*. What's gotten into *you?*"

Dad winced at the frown on Moura's face. "I can't allow you to talk like that. Apologize to Moura."

"For what? I didn't say anything to her."

Grabbing my shoulders, Dad said, "I won't tolerate your jealous, spiteful behavior, Jen. Moura has tried her best to get along with you. I expect you to treat her with respect. She's done nothing to earn your animosity."

"Nothing? What about my kittens? Ask her where they are, ask her what she did to them."

Dad frowned. "They were feral cats, Jen," he said slowly. "They've gone back to the woods. To their home."

Moura nodded. "Once feral, always feral. Dangerous, untrustworthy, ready to turn on you in a second."

"You—"

"That's enough," Dad said. "Not one more word, Jen!"

Without looking at me, Moura poured two cups of coffee, one for herself and one for Dad. The two of them sat down at the table as if I were invisible and began discussing their plans for the day.

"Are you still taking Jen shopping?" Dad asked.

"Of course." Moura darted a wicked look in my direction. "What better way for two females to bond?"

"I won't—" I began, but was interrupted by what felt like a bite on my ankle. Startled, I glanced under the table. Three mice stared up at me, their whiskers atwitch. The aunties were reminding me of my reluctant promise.

"Of course you'll go, Jen," Dad said in a firm voice I didn't like. "I have some rewiring to do. Tedious work. I expect it'll take most of the day. I need peace and quiet or I might end up electrocuting myself."

"But—" Nippety-nip on my ankle—a little harder this time. Soon I'd be bleeding.

"No buts," Dad said, more firmly than before. "Moura's looking forward to it. She knows the best shops." Eyeing my faded T-shirt and shorts, he added, "You really do need some fashion advice. I haven't got a clue myself."

Moura tapped my wrist with her long crimson nails. "You won't know yourself by the time I'm finished with you."

I cringed, sure I saw more in that remark than Dad did. He simply laughed and said, "Now, now, Moura, let's not go to extremes. I still think of Jen as my little girl. I don't want her to grow up too fast."

"No need to worry about that," Moura said, regarding me with a slight smile—more of a sneer, really.

Chills raced across my skin, but my father sat there calmly finishing his coffee, oblivious to the true meaning of Moura's words.

"Dad," I said, but he was already out of his chair and rinsing his cup in the sink. I wanted to tell him everything, but the words wouldn't come. Someone had my tongue and it wasn't the cat.

Moura was still watching me, the sneer even more of a sneer now that Dad's back was turned. "We might as well get started, Jen," she said. "By the time we get to Charles Town, the shops will be open."

"Dad," I tried again. "Don't let—" But that was all I could manage.

He smiled at both of us as if he hadn't even heard my faint protest. "Have a good time," he said.

I ran to him and hugged him. "Don't make me go with that woman!" I blurted out.

To my shock, Dad yanked me into the hall and pushed me against the wall, holding my shoulders firmly. In a low, angry voice, he said, "Get this through your thick head. I love Moura. She's a wonderful woman, and I'm lucky to have her. If you do anything to ruin my relationship with her, I'll never forgive you. Do you understand?"

"Let me go," I begged. "You're hurting me."

Dad gave me a shake, something he'd never done. It was as if he'd turned into a stranger. Even his voice was different, cold and full of anger.

"Moura's right," he said. "I've been too easy on you. You'd better start showing me some respect. I won't have a daughter who behaves like this."

"Dad . . . Dad." I began crying. "What's she done to you?"

Instead of answering, he turned to Moura. "Take her shopping. Maybe by the time she comes home, she'll keep a civil tongue in her head."

Moura marched me down the hall and out the front door. Holding me by one arm, she opened the car door and thrust me inside, forcing me to share the seat with Cadoc. I tried to open the door, but she'd already pressed the lock button—the child-resistant kind that made it impossible for me to escape.

"Now," Moura said, "you're about to discover what happens to nosy, interfering little girls." The car accelerated, and we sped down the driveway and out onto the road.

Peering through the window, I saw three crows flying in a row parallel to the road. The aunties. Please, please, let them be the aunties.

I glanced at Moura, but she paid no attention to the crows. She stared straight ahead, her mouth set in a hard line, her long fingers gripping the steering wheel. Like his mistress, Cadoc kept his eyes on the road. He showed no interest in me. Or the crows.

Without looking at me, Moura said, "I suppose you think you were very clever helping Kieryn to free her brother. But none of you is clever enough to thwart me for long. The fairy brats are hidden where they'll never be found or released. I would have preferred to kill them, but their mother's spell of protection was stronger than I expected."

She turned to me then, smiling that cruel smile. "But you have no spell of protection to save you."

I returned her unblinking stare and said nothing.

"So what do you think will happen to you?" Moura asked.

My heart pounded, but I didn't answer.

"Well, dear," she went on. "As I see it, you're destined to die today under tragic circumstances, struck down by an auto when you run across the street into the driver's path. Mr. Ashbourne won't be able to avoid you. I'll weep and tell the police I tried to stop you, but you were too angry with me to listen."

Moura smiled. "It won't be the first time a willful child has died defying an adult."

I gazed out the window at the three crows. Despite their presence, I shivered. Suppose Moura's power was too great for them to overcome?

The witch drove steadily, calmly, her eyes on the road. "If you think your father will pine away with grief, I won't allow that to happen. No, I shall be his solace. We'll marry soon after your death." She glanced at me, her lips curved into that dreadful smile. "Unfortunately, the poor man's happiness will be short-lived. Once I have what I want, I won't need him anymore."

To hide my fear, I kept my eyes on the crows. They flew just above the treetops, keeping pace with the car. Please, please, don't fail me, I implored them.

20

MOURA BEGAN HUMMING an eerie tune, disquieting, strange, yet somehow familiar. I put my hands over my ears, but I could still hear it. Like her perfume, the tune made it hard to think. It filled my head till there was no room for anything else.

"It's not too late, you know," Moura said suddenly. "You can still save yourself and your father."

I looked at her fearfully. "What do you mean?"

"It's so simple, dear child. Give me the pendant. I know you have it."

"No," I said, remembering what Binna had told me. "I'll never give it to you."

Cadoc raised his head, disturbed, I gathered, by my loud voice.

"Ah," Moura said. "I suppose the fairy brat told you it's hers, and you, foolish child, believed her. The truth is, her kinkind stole it from my kinkind years ago." She touched the red pendant she always wore. "All that remains of my kinkind's former power is this—an inferior stone whose magic is unreliable at best."

Moura's fingers tightened on the steering wheel. "The fairy kind took the throne from us, the rightful rulers. Since then they have persecuted us, exiled us from our home, rained misery upon us. You now have the power to redress the wrong done to us."

Her head swung toward me like a serpent's, and her eyes glittered. "Where does your loyalty lie, Jen?" she asked softly. "With your father or with liars and tricksters?"

Moura's perfume filled the car. Confused and dizzy, I felt myself wavering. Dad deserved my loyalty. He was my father. I loved him. He loved me. I had to save him.

But Binna's words ran round and round in my head—Her *cannot get it unless ye give it to* her, her *cannot get it unless ye give it to* her. I resisted the urge to unsnap my pocket and give Moura what she wanted.

"Dear child," she said softly. "Give me what is mine, and I will give you what you deserve. Is that not fair?"

I tried to understand what Moura was saying. She'd give me what I deserved, she'd give me, she'd. . . . I shook my head, sure those words hid another meaning but too muddled to know what that might be.

If only I could open the window and let fresh air into the car. Maybe then I could think clearly. I pressed the button, but the window didn't move.

"Well?" Moura held out her hand. "The pendant, please—that's all I ask."

My hand burrowed into my pocket, and my fingers

closed around the pouch. I must give her the pendant. I had to. It was hers, not Kieryn's. Then she'd reward me and vanish. Everything would be exactly as it used to be, just Dad and me.

But just as I took the pendant from my pocket, three deer bounded into the path of the car. To avoid them, Moura swung the wheel hard, and the car veered off the road and struck a tree. The windshield shattered, and cool, fresh air filled the car, dispelling the perfume.

Horrified at myself, I shoved the pouch deep into my pocket and resnapped the flap. I'd almost given in to Moura. *Almost.* If it hadn't been for the three deer—the three aunties—I'd have ruined everything.

While I sat there close to tears, Moura cursed softly got out to check the car. Eager to hunt, Cadoc leapt out after her, but the deer were gone.

After a quick inspection, Moura called Cadoc. With a swirl of her gauzy black skirt, she reseated herself behind the steering wheel.

"Now, where could those deer have come from?" she asked in a voice laced with sarcasm. "Strange that three deer should appear at such an opportune moment."

I turned my head away and said nothing.

"No matter," Moura said. "Old is old. Those three are no match for me."

Gravel spun from the tires as she swerved onto the road and headed again toward Mingo. Unnoticed by anyone but me, three crows left their perch in the tree's branches and followed us all the way to the Dark Side of the Moon.

With Cadoc at her side, she dragged me from the car and marched me up the sidewalk. If anyone had been nearby, I'd have shouted for help, but the street was deserted.

She thrust me into the shop and locked the door behind us. In the dim light, the antiques loomed in the shadows. Here and there a mirror caught a ray of sunlight, reflecting a Chinese vase, a stack of old books, grim faces carved on a chest. Dust motes floated in the air.

Moura led me to the kitchen and sat me down at the small oak table. Cadoc lay down at my feet, as if to guard me.

"I think a cup of tea would be lovely, don't you?" Moura asked.

I shook my head, afraid to drink the sort of tea she'd serve me.

Ignoring my refusal, Moura busied herself filling a kettle. As she set it on the antique stove, she began humming the same eerie tune she'd hummed in the car, oddly familiar yet never quite what I thought it was going to be. Insistent, irritating, it drove my own thoughts out of my head.

Trying to ignore it, I looked out the window and saw three crows perched in an apple tree. Feeling stronger, I returned my attention to Moura and the simmering kettle. She'd set two cups on the counter and was waiting for the water to boil, still humming but tapping the counter impatiently with her long scarlet nails. The morning light illuminated the lines etched on her fine white skin, showing her beauty for what it was—harsh and brittle.

At last the kettle began to whistle. Moura filled the cups with boiling water and set them on the table.

"One for you," she said, "and one for me."

"I told you I don't want any."

"Oh, yes, you do." Moura stared into my eyes, holding my gaze like a snake. "Go on, Jen, drink it."

Unable to resist, I lifted the cup. But before it reached my lips, the shop's doorbell rang loud and long. Her spell broken, Moura muttered to herself and went to the door.

The second her back was turned, I switched the cups, an old trick but one I hoped would work. Cadoc growled softly, his breath warm on my bare leg. I shifted my position, but he moved with me.

I heard Moura open the door and say, "The shop is closed today. Perhaps you could return tomorrow?"

"Oh, dear, we've come so far. Can't you let us in, just for a little while? We've heard you have a wonderful collection of dolls and such."

Ever alert, Cadoc left the kitchen and followed Moura to the shop.

With shaking hands, I rummaged through Moura's purse, my fingers clumsy with haste, and found the glasses. Holding them behind my back, I went to the kitchen door and looked down the hall to the shop's entrance.

If I hadn't recognized Binna's voice, I wouldn't have recognized her. She was dressed in a stylish denim skirt and a mauve blouse, her hair perfectly set, her makeup expertly applied—the very picture of the sort of woman who shops in expensive stores and enjoys fancy coffee in stylish little cafes. Behind her, Skilda and Gugi were equally transformed.

"Surely you can shop elsewhere," Moura said, making no effort to be polite. "There are at least three fine stores on Third Street that open at ten."

"Oh, but they don't have what you have." Binna pushed past Moura, and Skilda and Gugi followed her into the shop.

"Where do you think you're going?" Moura tried ineffectively to block the aunties' progress. "I told you, I'm not open for business."

When Cadoc growled, Skilda pursed her lips as if she were whistling. I heard nothing, but the hound cowered, ears flattened against his head, and whined in pain.

Binna confronted Moura. "What will you do if we don't leave? Call the police?"

"I think not," Gugi said and giggled in a most unladylike way. Her attention focused on Cadoc, Skilda continued to whistle silently.

Enraged, Moura drew herself up tall and straight. Her long hair flowed over her shoulders and sparkled in the light from the open door. She was majestic, fearsome, powerful. "How dare you speak to me so rudely?" she cried in a clear, ringing voice. "Leave my premises at once!"

Ignoring Moura, Binna reached my side and whispered, "Do ye have the glasses, Jen?"

I nodded, afraid to hand them over with Moura so close.

Moura stared at the three aunties and suddenly laughed scornfully. "I know who you are," she said. "Demented old fairies, long past your prime, weak, silly, ridiculous. You're no match for me. Begone!"

Terrified, I expected the aunties to vanish and leave me alone with Moura. But Binna shed her disguise and faced the witch. Instead of the eccentric old auntie I expected to see, Binna was as tall and straight as Moura. Long silver hair swirled around her pale, ageless face. She wore a long, flowing green gown, as dark as an oak's leaves in the summer twilight.

"Ye will send me nowhere, lady!" Binna cried.

Awed, I darted into the kitchen and cowered behind the stove. I had no idea what would happen next, but I knew better than to be caught in the middle of it.

A moment later, I heard something. I peeked out and saw Moura and Binna raise their arms over their heads and begin to hurl strange words at each other. The air between them glowed green, purple, and blue. Fireballs shot back and forth. The shop's walls shook. Antiques toppled to the floor. China figurines fell from shelves and shattered. Glass ornaments exploded.

I closed my eyes, unable to bear the blinding flashes of light, and covered my ears to muffle the loud noises. Gugi and Skilda, in their familiar shapes, scurried into the kitchen, crouched on either side of me and whispered comforting words.

"Binna's got big fierce magic," Skilda told me. "Her be the strongest of us, not to be taken lightsome."

"It's the witch blood flowing in her veins," Gugi added. "It come from her old kinkind, way, way back in olden times afore the First Witch War."

Slowly, Moura began to weaken. Stunned, she lurched into the kitchen, away from Binna, and finally collapsed against the wall. Cadoc lay on the floor near her, unconscious or dead. I didn't know which.

Binna ran to me. "Give me the glasses, Jen!"

Moura watched with horror as Binna put them on and opened the cellar door. Making a huge effort, Moura lunged at the auntie. "Give me those glasses!" she screamed.

At the same moment, Cadoc staggered to his feet. Binna evaded Moura, but the hound knocked her down. The glasses flew from her face and landed a few feet away. While Binna struggled to fend off Cadoc, Moura flung herself at the glasses.

In a flash, Gugi and Skilda became mastiffs even larger than Cadoc. Teeth bared, they attacked the hound and drove him away from Binna.

"Get the glasses, Jen!" Binna yelled.

Caught up in the fury, I forgot my fears and dove for them. Somehow I managed to snatch the glasses right out of Moura's hands.

"No!" Full of hatred, she grabbed for me, but I was too fast. With the witch behind me, I ran for the cellar. Binna slipped through the door after me. She slammed the door in Moura's face and locked it with the bolt and a hasty spell.

At the bottom of the cellar steps, Binna settled the glasses firmly on her long nose. "Where be they, Jen?"

"Here." I ran to the trunk. "Moura locked it and put a spell on it."

Her face tight with worry, Binna crouched beside the trunk and chanted strange words. Her voice rose and fell. Sometimes she sang, sometimes she hummed, sometimes she moved her hands the way Moura had. But nothing worked.

"The spell be a strong one," Binna muttered.

Upstairs, the battle continued, shaking dust and cobwebs down on our heads. The mastiffs barked and growled. Something large, probably Cadoc, began hurling itself against the door. How long could Skilda and Gugi keep him and Moura from following us to the cellar?

The tune Moura had hummed in the car came back to me, the way songs often do. Suddenly, I remembered why it had sounded familiar—it was the same tune the witch had hummed as she wove her sealing spell on the trunk. I started to hum.

Binna turned to me. "That's it!" she cried. "Keep humming. I can feel the spell loosening."

At last the lock on the trunk broke and the lid flew open. With her eyes safely shielded by Moura's glasses, Binna lifted out the globes. Deftly she pulled out the corks and out popped Kieryn and Brynn, tiny things one moment, full-size the next.

"Get behind the trunk," Binna told them. "Cover your eyes. Don't look at the globes."

As the two huddled together, the cellar door burst open, and Moura and Cadoc rushed down the stairs toward us. The mastiffs were right behind them, growling and snapping at their heels.

Binna thrust one of the globes behind her. "Turn back!" she shouted at the aunties.

The mastiffs stopped, confused for a moment by Binna's command. One's head swung toward the other. "Traps," Skilda whispered.

Both mastiffs fled, but Moura was too eager for revenge to notice. "Kill them," she cried to Cadoc. "The fairy, the girl. Kill them both!"

The hound leapt at us, huge, full of wickedness, his sharp teeth gleaming. Binna's hand flew up in a strange gesture. "Cadoc," she cried, "take yer true shape!"

Cadoc instantly shrank into a rat. For a second, he stayed where he was, chittering on his hind legs, his red eyes aglow, his hairless tail twitching as if he still meant to attack. Then he dropped to the floor and scurried away.

On her guard, Moura stood at the foot of the steps. She was obviously tired but not ready to surrender. "Surely, Binna dear, you mean me no harm," she said softly. "We share blood kinship, you know."

She paused, gathering confidence from Binna's silence. "That wretched human child has the pendant that can take us home. Seize it from her and claim your rightful place among the witches. We shall honor you, respect you, reward you with riches."

"But what of the fairy girl and boy?" Binna asked. "What of the human child? What will happen to them?"

Moura's silvery laugh chilled my blood. "The fairies will remain sealed in the globes forever, not to be seen again." Then, turning her eyes to me, she added, "This one is mine. To do with as I wish. She has vexed Ciril and me far too long."

Binna seemed to consider Moura's words, her expression unreadable. A chill crept over me like a shadow. Surely the auntie wouldn't accept the offer.

Slowly, Moura began to advance, her body swaying like a snake's as she moved. She extended her hands. "Dear Binna," she murmured, "what companions we will be."

"Truly?" Binna stretched out a hand, and Moura came closer, sure of herself now.

"Truly," Moura echoed.

"Dear, Moura," Binna whispered. "I fear ye be . . . mistaken." With that Binna held up the red globe, its pattern swirling in a burst of magic light.

"No!" Moura recoiled, but it was too late. Still screaming, she vanished into the trap, and Binna quickly corked the spout.

"There, Mistress Witch!" Binna cried. "What think ye now?"

The globe buzzed and vibrated, flashing a bile green light so brilliant that it lit the darkest corners of the cellar.

"They say ye can't trust witches," Binna told Moura. "But don't be trusting fairies, neither, 'specially not them with witch blood in their veins."

Winking at me, Binna changed into her familiar self, strange clothes and all. She dropped both globes into their velvet bags. "It's safe for ye now. The traps be in their bags."

Kieryn and Brynn came out from behind the trunk, dancing with delight. Brynn shouted loud enough for Moura to hear. "Ye won't be ruling us'n after all, ye skitzy old hag."

"Ye gets to stay here forever and ever," Kieryn cried. "But not us! We be going home!"

Light flashed out of the bag, still bright enough to make our faces green. She hissed, she buzzed.

"Oh, ye be mad now, Mistress Cicada!" Kieryn laughed. "But there's naught ye can do about it. Us fairies be smarter than ye thought!"

Hearing the commotion, Gugi and Skilda came limping down the steps, their clothing torn, their hats askew, sporting a few cuts and bruises from their struggles.

Skilda moaned and leaned against Gugi, but Gugi grinned and gave her a little shake. "Never mind this 'un. She always were a whinger and a whiner. We give that wicked hound an injury worse'n any he give us."

To Skilda, she said, "Ain't nobody feeling sorry for ye. Not now when we got *her* trapped."

Gugi laughed. After a second's hesitation, Skilda gave up her long face and joined in the cackling. There were hugs then, and kisses, dancing, and singing. In the midst of it all, Kieryn held me tight and whispered, "Ye been a true friend, Jen. I'll not forget."

"Don't be celebrating yet," Binna said. "We got *her,* but *him* is still loose." She handed me the bags. "Do ye know how to operate a vehicle, Jen?"

I clung to the bags, terrified of dropping them. "I'm only twelve," I said. "You have to be sixteen to get a driver's license."

"License be pooked to blazes," Gugi said. "Can ye manage to vehiculate to *his* house?"

"Here's why I be asking," Binna put in. "Us'n can turn crow and fly there, but we canna carry them traps. If ye can operate *her* vehicle, ye can meet us there with the wicked things."

"It canna be so hard," Gugi said. "Whilst I were a crow, I seen great dumblings vehiculating along the highway. If dafties such as they can do it, what's to stop a smart 'un like yerself?"

"But—"

"But me no buts," Binna said. "Take them keys I seen on the table and vehiculate."

With that, all five of them turned into crows and flew up the cellar steps and out the front door. Lugging the bags, I climbed the stairs in the usual way and got the car keys. It was hard to believe Moura wasn't there to stop me. Angry buzzes from the bag told me she would have if she'd been free to do so.

As a precaution, I dumped both cups of tea into the sink and left the shop. I hesitated beside Moura's car, once sleek and shiny but now missing the windshield and a headlight, and badly dented. But I knew it still worked.

Looking to the right and left, I saw the mailman turning the corner at the far end of the block. Fearing he'd ask what I was doing, I got into the car and stuck the key in the ignition. Next, I did what I'd seen my father do hundreds of times—turned the key, shifted from park to drive, and stepped on the gas pedal. The car shot forward and knocked over a trash can left by the curb. Panicked, I turned the wheel and almost hit a tree on the other side of the street. Obviously, there was more to vehiculating than Gugi thought.

The mailman was coming up the sidewalk, dropping letters into door slots. It seemed to me he'd spotted my blunders. Aiming the car straight ahead, I pressed the gas pedal cautiously and shot past him.

I ran through a red light I hadn't noticed and narrowly missed hitting another car. Horns blasted, but I kept going, heading for the open road outside town.

It was then I realized I had no idea where Mr. Ashbourne's house was.

21

DRIVING WAS HARD WORK. For one thing, I had trouble seeing over the steering wheel—which was probably why I hadn't noticed that red light. I was scared to go fast, so cars kept passing me. Some blew their horns. One driver made a nasty gesture as he sped by. Curves made me nervous. Stop signs frightened me. The sun was in my eyes.

Suddenly, a crow appeared in the road ahead of me. I braked, swerved, and came close to hitting another tree. The crow turned into Gugi. She yanked open the passenger door and jumped inside.

"Ye great ninny bob," she cried. "Ye're going the wrong way. Don't ye know where *him* lives?"

Almost too angry to speak, I shook my head. "How could I? I've only been there once, and I was hiding under a blanket, so I couldn't see a thing. It was dark when we left and I was a bat or a squirrel, I can't remember which, but we didn't follow the road home, that's for sure."

Gugi scowled. "Ye're a feisty lip swatter, ain't ye?" Then she laughed, showing a mouthful of crooked yellow teeth, and slapped my leg playfully. "Don't pay me no never mind, human child. I know ye be doing yer best. It's just I gets snarky sometimes and speaks rough."

I guessed she meant it as an apology, so I asked as calmly as I could if she knew the way to Mr. Ashbourne's house.

"Shush!" Gugi raised her hand as if to slap me but thought better of it. "Don't be saying that name out loud for all to hear. It be bad luck."

"Sorry."

She frowned and sighed and muttered something about dimbob humans. "Now," she said, "be quiet and listen and I'll tell ye the way."

Gugi directed me through a series of rights and lefts, up hills and down, through woods and over bridges, past cows watching us moodily from green fields. At last, Gugi cautioned me to slow down and park on the side of the road.

Four crows were perched in a row on a fence. When they saw Gugi and me get out of the car, they shed their feathers and wings and became themselves again.

"Jen's got no talent for vehiculating," Gugi said. "Nor does she have a skill at navigating. She were not only heading the wrong way but bouncing from tree to tree, making a big whumpus on the road."

"I never—"

"Hush, it be of no matter," Binna said. "Ye're here now, whumpus or no whumpus. Ye must all listen and do as I say."

Brynn frowned at Binna. "Who said ye were the boss of me?"

Without giving her aunt a chance to answer, Kieryn poked her brother hard with her elbow. "Hush up, ye pishy fool, and do what Binna tells ye."

To the rest of us, she said, "He thinks because he's a prince he gets to be boss. The big billybop—he'd still be in yon trap if it weren't for me 'n' Jen."

Brynn glared at Kieryn, but he had nothing more to say. At least for now. He was the kind of boy who made me glad I had no brothers.

"Now, as I were saying," Binna went on, shooting Brynn a nasty look, "I aims to change Jen into an old man and send her to the house. She'll take the bag with the empty trap, and that creepity-crawly Simkins will come to the door."

Binna turned her eyes to me, holding me fast with her stare. "Tell Simkins ye've heard his master collects witch catchers and ye've got one ye think he'll fancy. Hold up the bag so he'll see it's true. *Him* will come to look, wearing them spectacles."

She paused and gazed even more deeply into my eyes. She didn't blink, and neither did I. "This be the dangerous part, Jen, but I know ye can do it. Ye're made of brave stuff, child."

Binna took a deep breath. "Ye must pull the spectacles right off his nose. Quickly quick, show him the trap. In he goes. Plug up the spout bang-o and shove the trap back in the bag. We'll come then to help ye with Simkins."

Brynn sneered. "Ye're letting a human girl do that? Ye're mad, dafty, out of yer craney. Gimme them glasses ye took from *her* and let me be the old man. I'll be better than a dim-bob girl."

Kieryn gave her brother a shake. "And just what do ye speculate *him* will do when *him* sees ye wearing *her* spectacles?"

Brynn pulled away, pouting. Once more he had nothing further to say.

I was scared, but I don't think anyone knew it. I stood still and let Binna work her magic on me. In a few seconds, I was stooped and wrinkled. I had a beard. I leaned on a cane. My coat and trousers were ragged and dirty, and my shoes had holes that showed my toes.

"Oh, ye've got the skill, Binna," Skilda exclaimed. "Just look at the human child—an old man if ever I seen 'un. Don't Binna's magic shine yer eyes out, Gugi?"

"Aye, it do, it do indeed. She be the bestest of us three. The veriest queen of spells and magic."

"Go now," Binna said. "And be brave . . . be brave."

Clutching the velvet bag, I hobbled up the road. I looked back once at the fairies, but all I saw were five black crows perched on a fence. Two were smaller than the others. I walked on, alone and scared.

At the top of the hill, I stopped and looked down on the green lawn surrounding Ashbourne's house. Its towers caught the sunlight, its windows sparkled. His dark van sat in the driveway, ready, I supposed, to run me down in the street.

With slow steps, I made my way down the hill and up a

shady, tree-lined driveway. Trying not to tremble, I reached for the huge brass knocker and let it fall against the door with a loud thud. In a moment, I heard footsteps approaching. The knob turned and the door opened. Simkins stood there, scowling at me.

"We don't give nothing to beggars," he said. "Get out of here, before Mr. Ashbourne gives you a beating you won't forget."

Quickly I thrust my foot in the door, hoping it worked in real life as well as in books. "Wait," I cried in a hoarse, old man's voice, "don't be so hasty. I have something your master will want."

Simkins hesitated, the door open a slit as wide as my foot. "What could a bum like you have? My boss is a rich man. He don't need junk from beggars."

I reached into the bag, pulled out the witch trap, and held it up, willing my hands not to shake. "I've been told Mr. Ashbourne collects these. Isn't this one a beauty?"

Simkins sighed, obviously annoyed. "Wait there. I'll tell him what you got."

I stood in the doorway and watched the man disappear into a shadowy hall. Behind me, several crows cawed. I turned to see them perched in a tree, their backs to the house.

Soon Ashbourne appeared, eyes hidden behind his tinted glasses. "You have a witch catcher, I believe?"

I held it up, its colors brilliant in the sunlight. "A rare

find," I said, hoping he'd miss the tremble in my voice. "Only a few in existence, sir."

"Hmm . . . yes. I've seen only one like that." Ashbourne leaned toward me to get a better look at the trap.

With a speed I didn't know I had, I grabbed his glasses and flung them onto the grass.

Taken by surprise, Ashbourne cried out and tried to turn his head away. He was too late. In a flash, he was sucked through the spout and into the trap, buzzing louder than cicadas on a hot summer day. Green light flashed like flames, even more blinding than Moura's, and the glass burned my hands. Despite the heat, I managed to jam the cork in place and thrust the trap into its bag.

Simkins ran toward me. "Look what you've done!" he yelled. "Let him out, let him out!"

I ducked away, and at the same moment, five crows flew at him, pecking his face, beating him with their wings, drawing blood.

Simkins stumbled backward, shielding his face with his arms and cursing. The crows' loud caws deafened me, but I held fast to the bag and the furious warlock inside.

Drawn by the noise, Rose cowered in the doorway, her eyes huge with fright, and stared in horror at Simkins, who crouched at my feet, convulsed with fear.

"Stop!" the man begged. "I just did what I was told to do. He was my boss—blame him, not me."

The crows drew away from Simkins. Wearing her long

green gown, her silver hair shining, Binna towered over him, her face stern.

The man looked up at her, his body rigid with fear. Rose cried out and hid her face.

"Don't ye be afeared," Binna said calmly. "I've come to grant yer wish. Remember what *he* promised ye?"

"Eternal life," Simkins whispered, his eyes lighting with hope. "That's what he promised."

Binna glanced at Rose. "Were ye promised the same?"

Rose made a sort of curtsy, braver now. "Yes, ma'am, the boss gave us both the same deal. No wages for our work—just eternal life."

"I hates to see a promise broke," Binna said. "We fairies have our honor, ye know."

I stared at her in disbelief, but the fairies seemed to be amused. In fact, Gugi had covered her mouth to hide her grin.

Binna raised her arms. "Are ye sure ye truly want to live forever?" she asked.

"Oh, yes, yes," they cried out. "Eternal life!"

"Fair is fair, I say." Binna drew herself even taller and threw back her head. Her silver hair swirled in the sunlight, and her green gown shimmered like leaves in a summer breeze. "Simkins and Rose, from now and forever . . . be crickets. Creep and hide in dark places, never see the light of day, never speak in human tongue—but live forever."

As she spoke, Simkins and Rose vanished. In their place, two black crickets scurried across the floor, chirping in tiny voices. I watched them disappear under a carved oak chest in the entrance hall.

Binna laughed. "Aye, the two of ye will have all eternity to rue the day ye wished for immortality!"

Turning to me, she was herself again, a bent woman with bushy pink hair wearing a polka-dot dress and sagging striped stockings. "I reckon that'll do it for them two."

Brynn tugged at Binna's arm. "Take me home," he said. "Right now—splickety-split."

Binna frowned at the boy. "That's all ye can say? Ain't ye got a word of thanks for Jen here?"

Brynn shrugged. "She just done what she was told. That's no reason to thank her. And besides, she be a girl, a *human* girl without a drop of royal blood in her veins."

Kieryn cuffed her brother's ear. "I'd forgot what a spoilt brat ye be. Maybe I should've left ye in the trap and taken meself home without ye."

"Our mam would skin yer eyeballs if ye did such a tomfool thing as come home without me," Brynn said. "I'm to be king someday, in case ye forgot."

"King or no king, ye ain't worth the bother of talking to." Kieryn turned her back on him.

"Upon my red tenny shoes, that boy needs to be took down a bit," Skilda murmured to Binna.

Binna winked at me. "Don't ye worry. Ye can bet he won't be prating so biggety big with me around. I'll settle his royal nonsense quicker than quick."

"Maybe we could change him into a beetle or sommat

even worse," Gugi said. "A roach, maybe. Or a maggot. That'd humble him for certain."

Brynn looked at his aunties. I thought he might say something nasty, but he changed his mind. Keeping his mouth shut tight, he put some distance between himself and the three old ladies.

"All right," Binna said with a clap of her hands. "It be time to start our journey home." She glanced at me. "This time I'll do the vehiculating, Jen. Not that ye done a bad job getting here, child. But, well, we don't want no snog-whistling coppers stopping us, now, do we?"

Believe me, I was happy to crawl into the little back seat of Moura's car. I'd had enough of driving for one day—and many more. I set the bags carefully on the floor between my feet. Green lights glimmered through the velvet, but the buzzing had dropped to a low, tuneless hum.

Kieryn and Brynn squeezed in on either side of me, and the aunties wedged themselves into the front seat.

Binna wasn't much more skillful at driving than I was, but at least she could see over the top of the steering wheel. When we backed up instead of going forward, Brynn insisted he should take over the vehiculating, but Binna stepped on the gas and shot forward so fast we were thrown back in our seats.

"Dimbob booby," Brynn muttered. "How will she get us home? She be a melonhead if ever I see'd one."

Kieryn leaned across me to cuff Brynn. "Shut yer big boshy mouth. Binna be a fairy of the third degree, and if ye don't watch out, she'll spell ye, just like she done them two mortal fools."

"She wouldn't dare," Brynn said. "I be the future king."

"Ye don't know what I might dare," Binna said, "if ye keep on with that king clappetytrap."

Unfortunately, Binna turned to scowl at Brynn. The car ran off the road and bounced along the edge of a fence, knocking it to pieces and startling a bull. I looked back and saw him rampaging down the road behind us, obviously aggrieved. Before the bull caught up with us, Binna regained control, and once more we were zooming toward home and the tower, the traps unbroken in their velvet bags.

After a few near misses involving a tractor, a hay wagon, and a flock of hysterical chickens, Binna parked the car in the woods behind the tower. The setting sun hovered above pink and crimson clouds, and dark shadows thickened under the trees.

"Carry them traps to the tower," Binna told me. "But dinna let yer father see ye. The rest of us'll be crows—we'll meet ye at the top."

In a moment, five crows flew up into the air and headed for the tower, black shapes against the rosy sky. Weighed down by the two bags, I clambered uphill after them, stumbling on roots and tangling my feet in vines and brambles. The bags grew heavier with every step. Inside, the trapped witch and warlock buzzed louder. Soon I could make out Moura's voice.

"Ignorant human child, you'll be sorry. Just wait and see."

"Be quiet," I told her. "Nothing you can say will change anything. You're trapped now, and so is Mr. Ashbourne."

"You'll soon beg for my help," Moura hissed.

"You're the one who should beg," I said. "*I'm* not trapped. *You* are."

She laughed. "We'll see who's trapped, dear, we'll see who begs. Those who put their trust in fairies soon regret it."

22

ANGERED, I GAVE MOURA'S bag a hard shake. She cried out in pain, and I shook it harder. "You be quiet!"

Her voice subsided into an angry hum. Struggling with the weight of the bags, I climbed to the top of the hill and paused at the edge of the woods. It was dark enough now for Dad to have turned on the kitchen light. I saw him come to the door and look out, then return to whatever he was doing—cooking dinner, probably. He must be wondering where Moura and I were. Whom did he miss more, I wondered, her or me?

I hesitated, tempted to run home and tell Dad I was all right. A chorus of caws stopped me. On the tower's roof, five crows perched, obviously waiting for me.

I crept from the trees into the bushes at the tower's base. Sure that Dad hadn't seen me, I opened the door and dragged the bags up the steps. At the top, I stopped to rest, breathless from the climb.

Five crows flew into the tower through a broken window. Pigeons stopped cooing and huddled together on the rafters. Mice scurried to their hiding places under the dusty eaves. A book fell from a table with a thud, and a squirrel dashed for the safety of the ivy outside the windows.

The crows shed their feathers and wings and resumed their own shapes.

"Ye took long enough," Brynn said. "We been awaiting ye on the roof, watching for trouble."

"The bags got heavier and heavier," I said, still breathing hard. "I could barely carry them. I was sure I'd drop them coming up the steps."

"That's *her* doing," Binna said in a voice so fierce the bags buzzed. "Even in that pisky trap, *her*'s got power."

"Did *her* speak to ye?" Kieryn asked.

"Yes." I studied Kieryn's funny little pointed face and her odd slanted eyes. "She said . . . er . . . she said not to—" I couldn't bring myself to say Moura had told me not to trust Kieryn and the others. "Oh, it was just more of her lies and tricks," I ended up saying.

Kieryn looked at me closely and smiled a strange little smile. "I reckon *her* told ye not to trust us. That's the sort of thing *her* says about our kinkind."

I nodded, embarrassed, but I noticed the aunties exchanging odd grins. Brynn covered his mouth with his hand, but I heard him giggle.

"What did ye say to *her?*" Binna asked.

"Did ye believe *her?*" Kieryn asked at the same moment.

I was beginning to feel uneasy, almost afraid, but I looked Kieryn in the eye and said, "Of course I didn't believe her."

Turning to Binna, I added, "I didn't say anything. I just gave the bag a good hard shake to shut her up."

"Ah, that's just what *her* wanted ye to do," Binna said. "*Her* was hoping the glass'd shatter and *her*'d be free."

"Dimbob," Brynn muttered to me.

"Hush, boyo," Gugi said. "Yon human child don't know what we know, now, do she?"

It must have been a trick of the light, but for a scary moment, I thought Gugi winked at Brynn.

"Give me the pendant." Kieryn held out her hand. "Please."

I unsnapped my pocket and pulled out the little pouch. Kieryn watched me untie the string and remove the pendant. "Here," I said, relieved to be rid of it.

"Thank'ee for keeping it safe." Kieryn dropped the silver chain over her head, and the stone came to rest on her chest. The delicate star glimmered in the stone's deep blue depth.

"Come now, we be wasting time," Binna said. "We must decide what's to be done with the traps—and them inside 'em."

Binna put on the tinted spectacles and took the bags. Gugi donned the second pair, and the others turned their backs so as not to see Binna lift out the traps and set them on the table.

I watched Binna grow tall again, beautiful, powerful—and frightening. In awe, I stepped backward and bumped into Brynn.

Muttering "Dimbob human," he gave me a sharp pinch on the arm.

Binna's long green gown rustled as she leaned over the traps. She began to wave her hands as if she were shaping the air into unseen forms, just as I'd once seen Moura do. At the same time, she murmured in that secret language of hers. Gradually, the buzzing from the traps faded into silence. The green lights flickered and went out. Two glass globes lay on the table, their surfaces swirling with color, still beautiful but soundless, motionless.

"Did you . . . did you kill them?" I whispered.

"Nay, I do not have the power to destroy them two." Binna dropped the globes into the bags and sat down. In a moment, she was herself again, all grandeur gone. Her face pale, her eyes shadowed, she looked exhausted. "I put them under the strongest spell I know. It should hold *him* and *her* for many years—hundreds, maybe even thousands."

"As long as no billybop human idiot breaks the traps or pulls out the corks," Brynn added, giving me a sharp look.

Binna handed the velvet bags to me. "These I put in yer care, human child. Hide them away in a place where no one will find them—deep in the earth." She rose and walked slowly to the top of the steps. "Come, Gugi, Skilda, Brynn, Kieryn. 'Tis time to say farewell and be on our way home."

"But I thought Jen were coming with us'n—" Brynn began.

Binna gave Brynn a little pinch. "Hush yer mouth, foolish fairy," she hissed. "Jen ain't going nowhere."

Brynn rubbed his arm and scowled at Binna. "That hurt!"

"It were meant to." Binna leaned toward him. "And don't forget—there's more where it come from, boyo."

Edging away from his auntie's reach, Brynn said, "Me and Gugi and Skilda say aye to taking Jen with us'n."

"After she hides them skitzy traps, of course," Skilda put in.

I stared at Brynn, surprised by his unexpected friendliness. "You want *me* to come?"

He nodded, and Gugi and Skilda smiled. "Oh, aye," they chorused, "Come with us, human child."

"We wants to reward ye," Brynn added. "For all ye done."

Binna's face was expressionless, but she regarded me with mournful eyes. "It be yer choice, Jen," she said softly.

I turned to Kieryn. "What about you?" I asked. "Do you want me to come?"

Kieryn stood apart, gazing out a window at the darkening sky. She twirled her pendant slowly. The stone caught the last light of the sun and cast a colored shadow on the floor. Without looking at me, she shrugged her thin shoulders. "Like Binna says, it be yer choice."

"Come with us. Ye'll be glad if ye do." Brynn grinned at me like a small fox. "Our world be far more beautiful than yers. Happier, too. Nothing to trouble ye there. Nothing to sadden ye. We dance and play and never sleep. Feasts every night. All ye can eat and drink. Sweet desserts such as ye never tasted in this world."

Lovely as it all sounded, I didn't quite trust Brynn's smile or the mischief in his eyes. Up till now, he'd made it clear he didn't like me. Why had he suddenly changed? Something was wrong; I sensed it, but I hated to miss the chance to see Kieryn's home.

I looked again at Kieryn. She stood as before, gazing out the window, twirling the pendant. Tension tightened the air between us. Why was she so silent? Didn't she want me to go home with her? Had she turned against me?

Gugi took my hand. "Come with us'n, Jen. We'll show ye the olden dances and teach ye the olden tongue. We'll crown ye with jewels and gold. Soon ye'll forget this world of sorrow."

"But my father," I said. "What will he do without me?"

"Yer father betrayed ye." Skilda seized my other hand. "He cared more for *her* than he did for ye. He don't deserve ye."

Gugi held my hand even tighter. "Come, go with us, human child. We'll love ye more than any mortal could ever hope to."

Skilda was right. Dad had treated me badly. But Moura's magic and spells had blinded him, changed him. Now that she was gone, he'd become his old self. He'd love me the way he used to. How could I leave him? And Tink?

"Can I come for a visit?" I asked Gugi. "Just to see if I like it? And go home any time I want?"

"Why, that be a fossicking good idea," Gugi said. "Ye come now, and leave when ye tire of feasts and sweets and dancing."

She and Skilda swung my hands in theirs, smiling at me and each other. "Human child, human child," they sang, "come with us to fairyland."

Once more I turned to Kieryn. At last she met my eyes, "Are ye sure ye want to go, Jen? Think careful afore ye answer."

I stared at her, puzzled by the note of warning in her voice. "As long as it's just for a visit."

Kieryn whispered, "Do ye not recall what *her* told ye?"

I stared at her. "But Moura lied. You said so yourself. She's a witch."

"And we be fairies. Ye can't be trusting either one."

Brynn ran to Kieryn. "Hush! Hush! Ye'll ruin everything, dimbob!"

Kieryn pushed him away. "Ye beastly boyo, do ye not care that Jen saved us? Were it not for herself, ye and I and the aunties would all be swinging in them pisky traps forever and a day whilst *her* and *him* found their way home and seized the fairy throne."

"But we need a human child," Brynn said. "We've always took them. Never has a fairy said we should na steal 'em."

"Hush." Gugi gave Brynn a good hard swat on his bottom, and Skilda took my hand again. "Pay no mind to the boyo. No harm will come to ye in our world."

"No, indeed," Gugi said, once more taking my other hand. "And if ye miss your father, all ye need do is say ye want to go home, and off ye'll go, back to this troubled world of yers."

Kieryn pulled me away. "Stop yer ears, Jen. Ye mustn't listen to the aunties' stories. Fairyland's not what ye think."

"But I can go home if I don't like it. Gugi said so."

"Oh, sure ye can, Jen." Kieryn's voice brimmed with sarcasm. "Sure ye can." She scowled at Gugi who seemed to have lost interest in everything but the wart on the end of her nose.

Turning her green eyes back to me, Kieryn said, "Fairy time be different from yer time. What seems a day to us can be long years in yer world. When a mortal goes back home, he seeks things that be gone—his home a ruin, his friends and loved ones long dead, himself so old he soon dies and turns to dust."

"Now ye've gone and ruined everything, ye big dimbob!" Brynn wailed. "Mam won't have no slavey to work in the kitchen. I'll be fetching and carrying as no prince should, and ye'll be forever sewing and mending. And the aunties will be washing and scrubbing till their hands turn red and rough."

Still weary from her spells, Binna spoke at last. "So ye see how it be, Jen. If ye go with us'n, ye can't never really go home. Or see yer father again. And ye won't be singing and dancing and feasting. Oh, no, ye'll be toiling day and night."

She glanced at her sisters, her eyes flashing. "Fie and fie again on yer tricksy ways. Ye should be ashamed of yer dafty lies."

Skilda and Gugi stepped away from me, their faces red.

"Ah, didn't *her* tell ye not to be trusting the likes of us?" Gugi asked me. "And didn't I meself warn ye?"

"Ye see, it be our nature to deceive," Skilda said with a smile and a shrug. "Truly, we canna help it—even if it be unfair to one as kind as ye."

"So Moura actually told me the truth about you?" I stared at the five of them.

"*Her* was only seeking to help *her*self by turning ye against us," Binna said. "So it weren't no virtue on her part."

"We must go." Gugi pointed at a window. "Time hangs waiting between day and night."

As the others turned toward the stairs, Kieryn hugged me. "My kinkind ain't good at thanks or farewells, but we don't forget them that's helped us."

With that, she ran downstairs behind the others. I followed them out of the tower and into the dusk-filled woods. Binna stopped at an oak that rose above the other trees. Its ancient branches thrust toward the stars.

Rising up tall and regal in her green gown, Binna spoke a spell in her language. Beside her, Kieryn lifted the pendant above her head. The star inside shone with a brilliant light, and a door in the tree's mossy trunk opened. Darkness as thick as a black cat's fur lay within.

Binna turned to me. "Ye may look, child, but do not follow us. There be no turning back when the door closes."

With Brynn in the lead, Gugi and Skilda ran through the door. They didn't even say good-bye.

Kieryn hugged me again. "Farewell, dear friend," she whispered. "I'll remember ye always and always, forever and ever." Giving me a quick kiss, she plunged through the door, crying, "Mam! Mam! I'm home!"

Without thinking, I started to run after her. Binna stopped me on the threshold. "One look," she said.

I peered through the door at the twilight world beyond the darkness. I saw a castle with tall towers, cozy cottages, gardens, green lawns, graceful trees hung with lanterns. Somewhere a flute played. The air was fragrant with flowers. A crowd of fairies ran to welcome Brynn, Kieryn, and the aunties. One stepped forward and opened her arms. She wore a gown spun of fabric as light as moonshine and glittering with jewels. In her dark hair, a wreath of gold glowed.

"Mam!" Kieryn cried. With Brynn close behind, she flung herself into the arms of her mother.

"The queen," I whispered, "the queen."

As if she'd heard, the queen smiled at me over the heads of her children. She held out her hand, beckoning me to join her. She was beautiful, kind, and good. She loved me, and I loved her. My heart ached to be with her, to be her child, her darling.

Just as I stepped forward, Binna shook her head. "No, Jen. Ye must stay with yer father and live yer life willy-nilly in yer world."

Then she stepped across the threshold and raised her hand. The door slammed shut, and I was alone in the dark woods.

"No! No!" I dropped the velvet bags, threw myself at the tree and beat on it with my fists. I pried at the bark till my fingers bled. But the door refused to open.

Exhausted, I sank down on the ground and cried. The fairies were gone. I'd never see them again. I was stuck in my human body forever—no flying or creeping or crawling, no magic. Just one dull, ordinary day after another.

23

I PICKED UP THE two velvet bags and walked slowly to the edge of the woods. A cool breeze touched my cheek, bringing with it the smells of fresh-cut grass and honeysuckle. Overhead, the Big Dipper tipped across the sky. A car passed on the road below, its engine humming. An owl hooted.

The lawn, dull in the ordinary moonlight of my world, stretched uphill to the house. From every window, lights shone like beacons to show me the way home. It was late. I'd been gone all day. Dad must be worried about me—and Moura, too.

Tink came bounding across the lawn. He circled me, rubbing against my legs and purring. Suddenly, he paused and sniffed the velvet bags. Tail puffed, he crouched and hissed.

I knelt beside him and stroked his back. "It's all right," I whispered. "They can't harm anyone now."

Tink slunk out from under my hand. Taking a few steps toward the house, he looked back at me, clearly urging me to follow him home.

"Okay," I said, "okay." Dangling a bag from each hand, I

crossed the lawn and climbed the back steps behind the cat.

The kitchen door flew open, and Dad rushed out. "Jen!" he cried. "Where have you been all this time? Where's Moura? Why isn't she with you?"

I hadn't had a chance to think up a good explanation, so I simply said, "She's gone."

"Gone?" Dad stared at me as if I'd lost my mind. "Gone where?"

"She didn't say," I told him. "She just left."

"But you must have seen which way she went." Dad looked frantically across the lawn, his eyes sweeping the dark woods.

"We were in her car," I told him. "Down there at the bottom of the hill. She told me to get out and then—"

Without waiting to hear more, Dad ran across the lawn and into the woods. I plunged down the hill behind him and caught up with him on the road. To my amazement, Moura's car was gone. A small pile of sticks and leaves marked the place where Binna had left it. Was Moura's shop an empty lot now? And Ashbourne's mansion a pile of stones? The air around me tingled with magic, and I shivered.

Dad turned to me. The moon had risen above the trees and our shadows were black. "Are you telling me Moura left you here and just drove away?"

"That's what it looks like, doesn't it?" It sounded impudent, but I was trying not to lie.

Dad shook his head. The moonlight on his face showed

his anger. He seized my shoulders and shook me. "Why? What did you do to her? What did you say?"

I clutched the bags and stared at my father in disbelief. Moura was gone, but her spell on Dad hadn't been broken. Not yet, at least. "Let go," I cried. "You're hurting me!"

Slowly he relaxed his grip on me and sighed. "Surely she'll come back," he said. "She wouldn't leave, not like that, without even saying good-bye. She—" At a loss for words, he stared at the empty road as if he expected to see Moura's sporty car come purring over the hilltop.

"We were going to be married, we were so happy, we—" Dad's voice trailed off again and he stood there, head down, hands in his pockets like a disappointed child. "I don't understand," he muttered. "I don't understand."

The little pile of sticks and leaves lay between us. To Dad, they were nothing but roadside rubbish. Even if I told him what they were, even if I told him what had really happened, he wouldn't have believed me.

I touched his arm. "I'm sorry you're sad." I wanted to say more, much more—including *I told you not to trust her*—but I kept my thoughts to myself. Dad had been foolish to love Moura, but she was gone now, and the danger was past. He'd never know what she was or where she'd gone.

"Thanks, Jen." Dad gave me a little hug and trudged up the hill toward the house.

I followed, lugging the bags. Later, I'd bury them deep in the earth where no one would find them. But not now. I was much too tired. What I wanted more than anything was to crawl into bed and sleep for a week, maybe more.

At the kitchen door, Dad paused and looked back at the yard, at the glittering stars and the moon, at the dark woods we'd just walked through.

"I wonder where she is," he said softly, more to himself than me, "or if I'll ever see her again."

Inside one of the bags, I heard a tiny buzz—more of a murmur, actually. Alerted, Tink rubbed against my legs and mewed. When I looked down at him, he nipped my ankle gently, as if he wanted to remind me that glass breaks easily.

"What's in those bags?" Dad asked, noticing them for the first time.

"Just something I got from Moura," I said uneasily.

Dad reached for the bags. "Can I see?"

"Be careful," I said. "They're fragile."

Dad untied the drawstrings, took the traps from their bags, and laid them on the kitchen counter. Their colors swirled and sparkled, crimson and gold and deep midnight blue. One made a small humming sound that only Tink and I heard.

"Witch catchers," Dad said. "I'm surprised Moura would give these to you after all that fuss about the one you broke. She must have meant them as a peace offering. Maybe she's coming back, maybe she'll call, maybe. . . ."

He regarded the traps solemnly. "I have the oddest feeling Moura is somewhere nearby."

To my dismay, he picked up the one that held Moura. For a moment, the globe teetered in his hands and then rolled off his palms, arcing toward the floor and certain destruction.

With an agility I didn't know I had, I caught the trap just before it hit the tiles. "Dad," I cried, "how could you be so careless?"

"I'm sorry, Jen. It's almost as if the globe moved by itself. I couldn't keep a grip on it."

"It's okay." Keeping my hands steady, I put the traps carefully into their bags and knotted the drawstrings tightly.

Dad laughed. "Maybe that one has a real live witch in it."

I forced myself to smile at his joke, but what he thought was funny was nothing to laugh at. "I'm tired. Do you mind if I go to bed?"

"Go ahead. Tomorrow we can talk about what you and Moura did today, what you said to each other. There must be some reason. . . ."

Leaving Dad at the kitchen table, a cup of coffee going cold in front of him, I went upstairs. Before I got into bed, I had to find a safe place for the globes. The bottom drawer in my bureau was almost empty, so I made a little nest there with a couple of old T-shirts. I picked up the bags, but instead of putting them in the drawer, I opened them and peeked at the globes. Their colors glowed like jewels in the lamplight.

So beautiful, I thought, too beautiful to hide away in the dark. Surely I could hang them in my window for a few days and enjoy their colors in the sunlight and the moonlight.

I carried the traps to the window. Dad had been careless, but I'd hold them tight. I'd make sure they didn't fall and break.

The ribbon I'd used to hang Kieryn's globe still dangled from the curtain rod. As I reached for it, Moura's globe began to hum that lovely, eerie tune of hers. What if I'd been wrong about her? What if I should have trusted her instead of the fairies? Hadn't Gugi and Skilda tried to fool me?

Suddenly dizzy, I leaned out the open window and peered down at the moonlit lawn. The tower's shadow stretched toward me. Beyond it, the woods were dark. No aunties stood on the grass below. No Kieryn, no Brynn. They'd gone back to their world and left me here, alone and unhappy.

I climbed to the windowsill, my head reeling, and stood there gazing into the night. With a globe in each hand, I raised my arms to the moon. The wind blew my hair back from my face. Moura's song filled my mind with images of Kieryn's world. Maybe I could still fly, maybe I could change into a bat again, or a bird. . . .

Just as I gathered the courage to jump, Tink leapt to the sill beside me. With a loud meow, he drowned out Moura's song. To keep myself from falling, I dropped the globes on the rug and caught hold of the curtains. As I tumbled backward into my room, the traps began to roll away. Tink stopped one with his paw, but the other went spinning out my door, flashing green light and humming.

Still dizzy, I ran after the globe and caught it at the very top of the stairs. For a moment, I thought I was going to tumble straight down to the bottom. Without dropping the globe, I caught the bannister with my free hand and saved myself. Weak-legged with fright, I sat down on the top step. The globe's surface was hot and slippery and hard to hold. Still trapped inside, Moura hummed her wordless song.

"You almost tricked me," I told her. "Almost, but not quite."

Taking a deep breath to calm myself, I stood up. My heart was beating at least twice as fast as normal. "You'll never get away," I whispered to her. "Never!"

The humming rose, and I could hear her words, urging me to leave this world of woe and go away with her.

"No," I muttered. "You can't take me to your world. The door is sealed against you."

To keep from hearing Moura, I thrust the shining globe into its bag and knotted the string so tightly I'd never be able to untie it. I grabbed the other trap, bagged it, and tied its string into equally tight knots.

I didn't dare wait till morning to bury the traps. It had to be done now—before Moura tried to trick me again.

With Tink at my heels, I sneaked through the silent house and out the back door. A light shone in Dad's window. I imagined him sitting in the easy chair beside his bed, thinking of Moura, missing her, hoping she'd return. Poor Dad—he'd never know what I'd saved him from.

I slipped through the shadows and darted across the lawn to the garden. Luckily, Dad's shovel still lay in the grass where he'd left it. I grabbed it and headed for the woods.

Burdened with the shovel and the bags, I hurried as fast as I could through the dark trees. The moon splashed the path with light and shadows. Things rustled in the leaves, twigs snapped. Overhead, branches swayed and sighed in the breeze, making a mournful sound. Tense with fear, I tripped on stones and roots but managed to keep my footing.

"You won't make me fall," I whispered to the bag in my right hand, Moura's bag.

Tink ran ahead, his cat eyes seeing in the night. Every now and then he looked back, as if to make sure I was still following.

When I came to the river, the moon shone on the water and lit the path. I walked slowly, searching for a good burial place. Not too close to the river, not too close to a tree. I chose a spot near a group of boulders and began to dig. When the hole was about three feet deep, I laid the traps carefully inside and buried them. Just to be safe, I pushed a heavy rock on top of the grave.

"There," I said to Moura and Ciril. "I'd tell you to 'rest in peace,' but I doubt you will."

Except for the loud chirping of crickets, all was silent. If Moura was humming, I couldn't hear her.

I got to my feet and brushed the dirt from my hands. Tink purred and rubbed against my legs. With a deep sigh, I picked him up and cuddled him close, warm and soft against my face.

"Thank you for all you did to help me get rid of Moura." I

gave him a kiss on the top of his head. "You're absolutely the smartest, most beautiful cat on earth."

Tink looked up at me and purred even louder. For a second, I thought he said, "I know it," but it must have been my imagination.

With a little twist, he jumped out of my arms. I picked up the shovel, and we trudged back to the house. Dad's light was out. I hoped he was sleeping well and not dreaming of Moura.

In the morning, I'd ask him to take me to the craft shop to get a drawing tablet and a set of colored pencils. Maybe that nice woman would be there. This time, I wouldn't drag Dad away for an ice cream. I'd let him talk to her as long as he liked.

AUTHOR'S NOTE

About fifteen years ago, I was wandering around a crafts fair in Frederick, Maryland, looking at this, admiring that, enjoying the summer day and the tempting aromas of funnel cake, Polish sausage, and pizza wafting my way from the food concessions.

A booth run by a glassblower caught my eye. Among the goblets, bowls, and vases were glass globes that swayed in the breeze. About the size of softballs, they sparkled in the sun. Fascinated, I drew closer to examine their swirling patterns of iridescent color.

I noticed each globe had a spout on the side. Turning to the glassblower, I asked why it was there.

He grinned. "Why, that's to catch the witch."

"The witch?" I stared at him, puzzled.

"These are witch traps," he explained. "In the old days, folks hung them in their windows. If a witch came to the house, she'd see that swirl of color in the glass. She couldn't resist coming closer to see the pattern better. Then—*poof!*—before she knew it, she'd be sucked inside through the spout. As soon as she was in the trap, somebody would stick a cork in the spout and there she'd be, shrunk down to the size of a bug and trapped forever."

He smiled again. "Unless somebody broke the trap, that is."

Naturally, I bought one, and hung it in the window of my writing room. It's been there ever since. It must be working, because I haven't been bothered by a single witch yet.

I've been trying to write a story about the trap ever since I brought it home. Now at last I have.